Artemio's Fire

The Volcano at San Miguel
Book 1

Jeremy Harmer

WAYZGOOSE PRESS

ISBN-13: 978-1961953017

Editor: Maggie Sokolik

Cover Design: Getcovers

Wayzgoose Press

Eugene, Oregon, USA

wayzgoosepress.com

Contents

The Beginning

ANSELMO GONZALEZ DE LUNA, plump and satisfied, untroubled by questions of belief, sat behind his metal desk fiddling with the keys on his ring, and remembered how Artemio's Fire had first appeared. He must have been, what—six or seven when his grandmother had got them all out of the house in the middle of the night? The earth was shaking beneath their feet and the picture of the Virgen del Campo was slapping ominously against the wall, as if she were angry about something. They had been visiting his father's mother who lived in the village of Tres Rios, so-called because three streams converged there and formed a watercourse which, in the rainy season, gurgled its way through the plain.

The village no longer existed, of course, and the three-stream river had long since evaporated away into the steam of the past. But when Anselmo was small, it was the best place in the world. The air was clean and clear, sharp on your skin to make you feel alive, conscious of the spirits all around you. His grandfather had cows, and two dogs, Blanco and Negro, though neither of them was either wholly one colour or the other. In the hot afternoons, lizards crouched motionless, absorbing the sun's pounding heat, only rousing themselves to scuttle into the darkness below stones when they felt a foreign footfall approaching.

Anselmo's grandfather would come and take Anselmo and his brother in a battered old truck that rattled and groaned over the dry rutted roads. These roads were impassable during the time of the rains, but otherwise ridged and holed in crags that the vehicle's designers had seriously underestimated. The boys would sit with the dogs on the flatbed behind the cab holding on for dear life, laughing with glee, while the dogs held their heads out as far as they would go and their long ears flapped around them like flags on Independence Day. When they got to Tres Rios, their grandmother would envelop them with her rough, lined love and spoil them as if she had never had any children of her own.

Sometimes at night, when the coyotes howled in the darkness or their room was lit by the megawatt scare of sheet lighting before great drumrolls of thunder rattled the windows, the boys would cry out in spite of themselves. Their father's mother, impossibly old and smelling of the foreign powder she was so proud of, would run into the room and take them into her own bed, evicting their grandfather to some other room while they snuggled into her surprisingly soft flesh. She would sing to them, tell them tales of old gods and new saints, and then they would feel safe because however loud the thunder crashed and however brightly the lightning picked out the crevices on the old woman's face, they knew they were protected.

But this night was different. There were no calming words now, no deep mattress with its enveloping serapes. Instead, they were pulled roughly from their bed—Anselmo by his grandfather, tobacco-stained and rasping against the young boy's cheek, and the smaller Gerardo pressed into his grandmother's loose bosom. Then they were outside, and now, as Anselmo remembered it, he saw the dark obsidian of the night sky lit by the heartbreaking brightness of a million glittering stars while below their feet, the earth swayed and buckled. There was a sound like the groaning of a great animal in pain and the hint of distant thunder. He looked around for Blanco and Negro. When he saw them they were half crouched, the elbow joins of their legs bent into sharp angles, their ears pressed flat against their heads as their eyes rolled in silent terror. Fenceposts creaked around them, yet there was no wind.

Then Anselmo's grandfather pointed. "Look!" he said in

wonder. "What in the name of all the gods is that?" The children were suddenly afraid because when their grandfather spoke, which was seldom, he never sounded as he did now, like a scared boy in an adult playground.

They followed his amazed stare and saw where a column rose into the sky some five or six kilometres away, blotting out the stars, and at its base, they could make out orange-red tongues of sulphurous fire.

"Mother of God", their grandmother exclaimed, "That's Artemio's land, Artemio's land. Poor man. In spite of everything." She crossed herself. But she need not have worried on his account. Señor Artemio, recently widowed, was away in San Miguel that night, visiting his whore. The arrival of a brand new volcano in the centre of the meadow below his farmhouse caused Señor Artemio no personal injury, but two campesinos who worked for him suffocated in the noxious fumes of the earth's gut and the eructations of magma, molten and corrosive, could be seen for miles around.

In the dawn, a cloud of thick dust hung in the air above Señor Artemio's land. Pools of molten pus steamed and bubbled around his farmhouse until it vanished completely in a blaze of fire and smoke. Days later, when the lava had lost its livid brightness, it still gave off intolerable heat. When their grandparents finally took them to look at what had happened, they had to stand a few hundred metres from the nearest lava channel. They still felt the scabrous breath of the world's intestines on their cheeks.

"Long ago," Anselmo's grandmother told them a couple of days after that as a distraction from their incessant questioning and obvious unease about the new volcano that was pushing itself out from the ground, "as I have told you many times, people believed in other gods." She was peeling the skins from the hot peppers she had just roasted on the rings of her primitive cooker. Even now, Anselmo could never smell the enticing aroma of burnt *rajas* without his grandmother springing instantly into his head.

"How long ago, Abue?" Gerardo piped up, rounding his childish consonants. "As long ago as before you?"

"Yes, child, even as long ago as that. Even before I was born. Long, long before that. In the old times. In those far off times," she

3

went on. "In this valley and in all the other valleys around, even as far as a man could travel, people believed in old gods from the old stories."

"What stories, Grandmother?" Anselmo encouraged her. "Stories of Artemio's fire?" The name had been instantly coined on that first night and now it was established so that the growing mound of solidifying lava would never be known as anything else.

"No, not exactly," she said ruffling his hair fondly. "That had not yet been seen. How could it since it was only a few days ago that this thing has happened..."

She paused, looking pensively through the window before straightening her shoulders, as if with an effort, and turning back to them. "Look, " she said, pulling them both to her. "This is the story of Tlalcoltepeca, a great god, all blazing eyes and ripples of dark hair. When he spat his saliva made great rocks. His breath came from his nostrils like smoke, and when he was angry, flames came from his mouth baking everything he breathed on into ash."

"Tlacoltepeca had a daughter called Xenal, who was everything her father was not. She was sweet, loving, pretty, and pliant. Her breath was not all smoke and fire. It had the scent of flowers in the spring, and her eyes glittered like stars. She was the one person who could pierce her father's craggy heart and he loved her with a fierce joy."

"One day, walking the fields, Xenal saw a beautiful man, tall and handsome, his hair golden, his body sleek and muscled. He smiled at her with a look that stretched from his chin right to the top of his beautiful head. She could do nothing but respond. When he took her in his arms she wept for the joy of it and was truly happy."

"When Xenal's father found out about her new boyfriend he went mad with rage. He was, after all, one of those fathers who think they own their little girls. No suitor could ever be good enough to match their own perfection. At least that is what they think that their daughters ought to think. Perhaps it was realising that this was not so which drove Tlalcoltepeca mad. At any rate, he told Xenal that she should never see the boy again. But she could not deny her new feelings of love, so one night she crept out of the house when her father was asleep and ran away with her new lover."

"What happened, what happened, Grandmother?" Anselmo cried, his boyish eyes shining.

"What happened? Well, you see, Xenal's beautiful lover was called Quatixtlaqueña. He was the sower of seeds. All he wanted to do was love his new bride and give new life to plants in the earth's waiting soil. Now, as they ran, Xenal's tears of joy watered his seeds and they grew tall. The ground became fertile. But when Tlacoltepeca woke up, he realised what had happened and pursued them. Every time he found them, he spat fire and death and made the earth shudder around them so that Quatixtlaqueña's crops should be destroyed. Now Xenal's tears were bitter, not sweet, and they flowed unstoppably, in great torrents, and the earth ran away in storms and cascades. Which is why, when it rained and the earth was irrigated, the ancient people said Xenal was weeping for joy, but when wind and rain laid waste to the ground, and storms caused havoc, they said it was Xenal's grief. When the earth erupted and volcanoes spouted their fire, then, according to those ancients, Tlalcoltepeca had found the runaways and was showing his anger by destroying their crops."

"Is that what you believe, Grandmother?" Anselmo asked. His brother beside him looked confused.

"No, of course not, child. Those are stories from the old times. We believe different things now. We are not crazy and superstitious as they were. Back then, they used to sacrifice young girls. They would throw them into sacred wells, hoping to take Tlalcoltepeca's attention away from his daughter. They thought that if they could tempt him with beautiful maidens he wouldn't spend all his time chasing the runaways. Then the two young lovers could plant and water their corn so that the earth would be full of great riches. It was all nonsense, of course."

She turned back to the cooker as if she had gone altogether too far.

"Well, if it was all nonsense, why is there a new volcano at Señor Artemio's ranch?" Gerardo said.

"I'm sure I don't know," his grandmother replied. "It is the Lord's will. Just as it was his will that Señor Artemio should be spared and that those two poor fellows should have been taken to heaven. If you two behave yourselves and are good, one day you will surely go to heaven, too, for you are the most beautiful children in this world and your grandmother loves you." She hugged them to her as if she might never see them again.

Now, sitting at his desk, remembering those days, Anselmo smiled to himself, a sad nostalgic smile, wishing he could talk to his grandmother again, or that he could bump over the rutted tracks with his grandfather, or sit outside the farmhouse staring up at the stars in the glistening black sky. But all that was gone, even if the volcano at Artemio's ranch had not. It had continued to erupt, creating more and more rivers of lava that flowed into each other and grew as they cooled. Then the authorities insisted that the inhabitants of Tres Rios and the surrounding villages abandon their homes and move elsewhere. Gradually, the land around Artemio's fire became covered in volcanic ash and the once verdant valley was redrawn as a black abandoned moonscape. At its centre, the fifty-year-old mountain strutted its muscular identity in the pride of its relative youth.

Well thank God for that, anyway, Anselmo chuckled to himself, because we have tourists now who buy the trinkets I sell—tin whistles and rustic toys, painted artefacts, and imitations of ancient pottery. Then he chided himself for bringing God into it, for in reality he did not believe in any deity. Luck, destiny, or accident seemed about the best explanation he had ever been able to come up with (he hoped the spirit of his grandmother could not read his mind).

He was lucky to have finally persuaded someone to marry him. Lucky he'd switched to toy-making (on a whim) when the silver business he ran with his brother had collapsed. Lucky that the town of San Miguel de las Colinas was to celebrate the fiftieth 'birthday' of their own volcano with a series of events, concerts, and marches. Everyone, it seemed, wanted to mark the half century of regurgitated magma. So no, Grandmother, he almost said to the memory of her, it is not your Lord's will, all this, and I don't believe in the old fire-spitting and earth-nourishing gods either. Living a pleasant and easy life in the contented arms of a wife, that's what I believe in. Let the others talk up the festival if they want: the cranky celibates at the town's elegant churches who preach the mercy of God if you can bear to wait for it, those shaven weirdos who were rumoured to be planning some cultish celebration at the crater lip, the white-hooded demonstrators with their belief in the dignity of human justice, the *musicos* with their melodies and concerts, the town authorities with their puffed-up civic pride. If they wanted to invest the celebrations with their own beliefs and desires well, why shouldn't they? As for him, he was looking forward to a period of healthy selling.

If Anselmo had known what was to befall his town and how the festival would, in later years, be remembered, he would at that moment have been less sanguine about the future. But then, as he himself might have said, that's the trouble with luck and destiny. You never really know how they are going to turn out.

Part One

The City Far Away

Martin

WHEN HE REALISED that he had finished, and that there was nothing left to write, Martin Caldecott was overwhelmed with a black realisation of loss. Behind him, the music coming from the radio seemed to have lost all its warmth. The sinuous melodies of the tune that was playing had flattened out and its exotic polyphony was neutered by his own inability to respond. He got up from his seat and wondered what he could find next to believe in.

Walking over to the sliding glass doors of his apartment, he pulled one back and stepped out onto the small balcony three floors up from the street. A car roared past below him, a monstrous black thing with its heavy disco beat thumping from vibrating doors.

Martin inhaled the fetid smell of the city—a sweet perfume of all its humanity, all the dust particles and noxious fumes smogged in its soupy excess. He reached into his right shirt pocket and took out a crumpled packet of cigarettes. Lighting one, he sucked in the dark sugar of its smoke.

There were human noises above the steady soundtrack of cars and buses and trucks on their way out of the metropolis, and the metro taking workers and revellers back home. The clatter of a million different air-conditioning systems throbbed in the balmy night. Over to his right, he could occasionally hear close harmony voices sneaking out from Las Fuentes restaurant. He thought of evenings they had spent there, the sweat of hot pepper dinners, the sharp tang of another Blanquita swishing down his throat, musicians standing around the table singing their hearts out. All that exaggerated conviviality chased the dragons away. It had seemed like living, then and now, even now. He supposed that it could still conjure magic from its clichés. But he had not been back there for an age, even though he had not moved from his flat which was close by. He was too nervous of its charms, too wary of its power to evoke memory, and too ashamed to absorb another reminder of loss.

In an apartment above him, to his left, he heard a woman's voice, shrill and insistent, raised in anger against whom—a rebellious daughter? An unsatisfactory husband? A clinging brother? (He grimaced to himself.) Or, just the release of frustration?

It could do that to you, this extraordinary city, overwhelmed by the heavy spring tide of humanity that struggled through its hot sweaty days and sad clammy nights. You either loved it or you hated it, he would tell visitors from far away. There's no in-between.

He himself loved it, even though he feared it, too. That's why he was still here a long time after he might have gone. It was the savage insistence that persuaded him, the memories, the way that the violence of his feelings matched the carelessness of the streets. He loved the history around him, both ancient and modern, sodden with heat and passion. It was never like this back home, he thought. Then he would remember that there was no 'back home' and that here was all there was.

He stubbed the cigarette out in the ashtray he kept on the metal table by the railing. He was overcome by an appalling ache of loneliness now that he longer had the characters in his writing to listen to or live with, however autobiographical they had been. *You should get out more,* he told himself, smiling at this use of a phrase he had read in a magazine only the other day. For some reason, he thought of their first holiday together, soaking up the sun in the resort at Siete Vientos, eating too much, drinking, and lazing in the Pacific. For a second, he could smell the brine and hear the call of the gulls and the putter of speedboats in the bay. But the more he remembered, the more he felt the emptiness expanding inside him to engulf him.

This is no good, he told himself, combing his hand savagely through his hair and biting his drawn-in bottom lip. *I'm getting maudlin again with that familiar cocktail of longing and guilt. All that looking backwards. Shit. Shit. I've got to get out.*

He went back into the main room. He recognised the track they were now playing on the radio. It had been one of his sister's favourites a few years ago, and it was often featured on the foreign station she worked for. "Sweet dreams are made of this," sang the vocalist. "Who am I to disagree?"

But, oh God, what am I looking for? he asked himself for the thousandth time, stranded here in an alien land which is as close to a home as he was ever likely to get. He picked up the phone. He knew the number by heart. When he heard the sleepy voice answer him he felt better. Who else, after all, did he have to call?

Maria

MARIA WATCHED her husband drive away, noticing the extra dent on the lid of the trunk. As she saw this, she thought how shabby the taxi had become. It lurched unnaturally as Juan sped off, all guttural engine racket and smudged exhaust fumes in the murky air. Years ago, she thought wistfully, you would have been able to see the mountains from where she was standing. But today, in the colder morning air, the smog cloud had trapped the dark summer in, and the air was impenetrable, keeping the sun from getting through to warm them.

As Juan disappeared, she looked around her. In the polluted gloom, she could see no further than three blocks. She already felt soiled by the particles of dust. Back when we were younger, she almost said aloud, I was thin and full of hope. I married my young man because of his smile and his swagger—and because I had always known I would. But now I'm all round and shapeless, and as for love (she felt for her bruised cheek), that has turned into something as filthy and contaminated as this town. Señor Jesús, have pity on me. He's a bastard, that man.

She turned away from the street. Reaching into the pocket of her smock, she pulled out the key ring that banged against her thigh as she walked. From along the street, where he was watering the sloping grass verge, the gardener from number 226 called her name and waved. Maria waved back. She liked that man. She selected the correct key and put it into the lock in the wire mesh. She opened the right-hand gate and went through into the garden beyond it.

Rusty, whose name she still found difficult to pronounce, bounded up to her, letting out a joyful series of barks. He jumped up at her as he always did, his tail wagging ecstatically from side to side, and as she always did, she fended off his advances, telling him in her sternest voice to get down. He gambolled along beside her, oblivious to her disapproval, as she made her way to the side of the house. She told him he was silly, too old to behave so childishly. She no longer felt embarrassed by the fact that she was talking to a dog. Some time ago, she had realised how nice it was to have someone—even an animal—greet her with such untrammelled enthusiasm.

At the side of the house she pulled back the screen door and let it bang shut behind her as she stepped into the kitchen. She noted with distaste the usual clutter of dirty plates and cups on the large table in the middle of the room. Breadcrumbs were scattered around like the first manifestations of volcanic ash. Ignoring the voices from upstairs, young and old, and the footsteps running backwards and forwards along the corridor above her, she turned right and went down the two steps into the passageway that led to the maid's quarters. Once there, in the dark little room, overflowing with washing that she would have to iron later in the day, she took off her coat. She took a pair of comfortable indoor shoes from her shoulder bag and dropped them on the floor beside her. Kicking off her outdoor shoes, she slipped her feet into the slippers.

She approached the mirror and studied her face. There were visible bruises. The swelling blurred the still-just-visible line of her cheekbone. She went back to her bag and took out more of the cheap cream she used. She took off the cap and, wincing in discomfort, she spread it on the thickly. She looked at herself again. Now, her face glistened. The bruising was less obvious. But some of them, Señora Bicky anyway, would notice her new disfigurement, however long it did or didn't last this time. She wouldn't be able to keep her face turned away all day.

¡Bendita Santa Maria! She could stand anything, even the hurt, but not this embarrassment. Why should she be the only one to carry these marks of shame? Why should she be the only one to carry the force of the pain which was inflicted so carelessly? Why should she have to endure any of this any longer? If she hadn't taken those vows all those years ago, she would not be so trapped. Surely they could not be broken, however pressing the cause. Or were some things simply no longer bearable?

Jacinto

Jacinto Perez, a professor and renowned violin virtuoso, combed his stubby fingers through the black curls of hair covering Angelita Hernandez' pubic bone until he could reach down and cup her wet sex in his importuning hand. She shifted on the disturbed couch beside him as, to provoke her further, he brushed his lips against her breast. He felt her awakening response shudder through her. To his immense relief, he felt himself stirring, too, and this time, he was suddenly confident that things would go all right.

He looked at the girl's sweet eyes—wide, fear-enhanced, and glittering with excitement. Surely, he told himself, this could not be wrong. Then he was worried as he could not remember whether he had locked the door. What if someone came in? They all suspected him of liaising with his female students, but no one had ever actually seen him do anything that he would have to explain later. He had always been too careful for that—for their sakes.

He felt his resolve weakening. It seemed to sense the slowing down of the blood-flow that he so urgently required. *Oh no,* he heard himself worry, *not now. Please not now.* Angelita shifted against him and, daringly, took his head in her arms and planted her warm lips upon his mouth. That did it. Or maybe it was the cloying scent of her engaged sexuality, or the tantalising satin of her trembling flesh.

He forgot about the door and his doubts evaporated, cauterised by the fire of his passion. When, seconds later, he climbed on top of her and felt the cushion slide of his entry, he thought he was in heaven, young again, pure of spirit, a dependent child, loved and sheltered, a poet, a weaver of melodies, a vulnerable conquistador, a man.

His beautiful student, womanly beyond belief but blessed with a young and valiant grace, moved gently beneath him, exquisite and overpowering. Now, with every exhalation of her perfumed breath, every tightening of his own replete arteries, he realised the sheer correctness of what he was doing. He understood, right down in the bottom of his belly and the heights of his brain, the nature of perfection. No one, surely, would dare to deny him this concerto of passion.

What was it, this penumbra of existence, if not the chance for experience, and the touch, *Dios mío*, of God's hand upon his brow to obliterate the tedium of life's relentless mandala? Just living, it seemed to him, happened predictably fast, the weeks and years accelerating past him into a garish fairground ride, scary, but lacking any real substance. Even music, the clasp of hair on string, the perilously held note, and the heart's vibrato that banished the quotidian, passed away too quickly. When it was over it was gone, dissolved into thin air. Few even remembered it.

That's why this was so different. Skin on skin. Plunging touch and held thighs. No one would forget this. I'll remember this, his insides shouted. I'll remember every touch and olfaction, every shudder and tremor. I'll hold on to this forever and ever.

When Angelita had first come to him, this child of twenty-two or maybe twenty-three, he had been immediately impressed by the profusion of tight black curls which cascaded down her back, and by the flash of her eyes. She was clearly nervous of him, but he was used to that. He prided himself on his ability to tease out the skill beyond the fear which inhibited so many of his young pupils when confronted with his fierce professionalism. Yet, when she started to play, he recognised immediately that he was in the presence of something special, something young and life affirming. There was an energy about her, a dedication unmarked by cynicism and expe-

18

rience, that he found immediately invigorating. If he allowed himself to feel, he told himself, he could weep at the arched beauty of the sound she made. But then he chided himself because he was entranced by her bowing arm, the ripple of young muscle, the fluency of her body, the way the flickering of horse hair across the strings lifted the material of her blouse, and the dreamy look that obliterated her features in those legato passages.

She was everything he yearned for himself, every resonance he regretted having left behind. *Hombre*, he told himself, *if I was twenty-five years younger!* Then, he offered her his advice, told her how she might enhance her technique at this point or that, or watch out for the pressure in bar thirty-three. She looked at him with an honesty that had left him temporarily speechless. When, for professional reasons only, he had put his hand upon hers to guide her bow as if it was his own, the shock of contact and a rush of electricity had made his legs wobble, taking the ground from under his feet. With that sweet sickliness he recognised as the kind of friend you wished you didn't have, he realised that he was about to become infatuated all over again.

Now he touched her face, kissed her eyes, pulled her legs around him to love her better, conscious with an enhanced precocity of the transitory nature of his life. He suffered the beauty of her presence, driven ever more urgently by the imperative of their mutual desire, harder and harder, until it seemed as if he would be parachuted into the sweetest, darkest abyss. He reached inside himself for a final exhalation of his being. He heard a creak behind him, the ratchet of metal. An ordinary sound—a door opening. Beneath him, the radiant violinist, lips stretched and parted, gasped in the excitement of approaching release. Behind him, he heard the sound of a groan escaping someone else's lips. An unmistakable sound. His son. He had opened the unlocked door to witness his father, unstoppably, reach his suddenly unwished-for consummation.

Martin

MARTIN CALDECOTT DID NOT KNOW that it was the music student Angelita he saw as the metro sashayed on its rubber wheels through the muggy evening some time later, but he knew at once that there was something special about her. He let his eyes rest upon her longer than might otherwise have been customary; he only turned away when he thought that his interest might be misconstrued. But he kept looking back at her, intrigued as much by her beauty as by the story her posture was telling as she sat there. To his surprise, it was a story he was suddenly eager to unravel. Except he never would, he told himself. How would he ever approach her, after all? Not only had he lost all confidence in his ability to charm anybody, but the girl herself was clearly unapproachable, locked in some private narrative which threw barricades around her.

She was about ten years younger than him, he judged. Her hair was pulled away from the sides of her face, held untidily by two tortoise- shell clips. He could not, from where he was standing, see her eyes. But, her dark brows arched the perfect circle of her fore-head, with its light skin above the strong nose with its exquisitely flared nostrils. She wore jeans and a blue Indian-style smock with coloured braids of rich seaming running from shoulder to waist on either side of its v-neck. Across her lap was a flat leather portfolio, and on top of that a case for some kind of instrument. She had a little leather bag hanging from one shoulder, its second strap dangling redundantly down at one side. Her hands rested flat on the case. Her short fingernails were unpainted.

An *albañil*, probably a plasterer to judge from his cream-spattered overalls, sat next to the troubled girl, his head lolling in sleep. On her other side, a large woman, old enough to be his mother, watched him over a pair of reading glasses, pushed low down her nose. When she saw that he was conscious of her enquiry, her mouth lifted and her top lip curled in sardonic amusement.

He looked away through the carriage window. He could see the wedge of traffic rattling down one of the city's main thoroughfares which ran alongside the train tracks. Some of the cars had sidelights on. Some were weaving in and across the various lanes in anarchic defiance of sense and safety. He became conscious of the heat around him and the smell of steamed flesh, and felt stifled. His shirt stuck to his shoulders and clung to the small of his back.

They slowed down. The line of cars that had seemed harnessed to them moved forward and out of sight to be replaced by a mass of other vehicles. There were great roaring lorries, buses with their stovepipe whirls of diesel smoke, and death-defying cars hurrying through the early evening. What would one of this country's old revolutionary heroes, resurrected after sixty of seventy years, make of this relentless stampede of metal and piston? How would one of the old viceroys from history evaluate this chaos? How had he allowed himself to become so used to it?

The train slowed into the station. He had to reach for the overhead strap to steady himself as the driver kicked in the hydraulic brakes too fiercely. The doors hissed and opened with a double clunk as they hit their restraints between the walls of the pale orange metro. The woman with the reading glasses pushed herself awkwardly to her feet, propelling her bulk upwards into the small passage between the seats. With a satirical look at Martin, she made her way through the stressed bodies and out onto the platform. He watched her straighten her skirt and remove her glasses to let them rest on the slope of her generous chest before she set off towards the exit steps and disappeared from his view. In front of him the woman's place was immediately taken by a young mother clutching bags full of baby equipment, her child half hidden where she clasped it tightly to her chest. It jerked its pink-hatted little head and let out a piercing scream and the sank back into sleep.

He saw the girl look up then, suddenly awake as if aroused from a bad dream. She gazed around her, saw the station name through the window and made to rise, her sad face suffused with a precarious urgency. She had to lunge forward to stop her instrument case from falling to the floor. But at that moment the metro started up again and she sank back, defeated.

In that brief moment of panic when she had looked up and realised where she was, Martin caught the full power of her beautiful eyes. They were light hazel brown, almond-shaped, delicate, but deep and suspended, it seemed to him, in some great trouble. She saw him watching her. He just had time to notice the wide mouth, generous-lipped and slightly parted, the shiny regular teeth, the strong chin and the spreading of a blush across her perfect cheeks before she lowered her head defiantly. She once again slumped, head bowed, as they rattled pneumatically along the long transport artery, travelling north across the urban moonscape he had learned to call home.

But for how much longer? he asked himself. Perhaps he should leave. There was nothing to hold him here. He'd finished the book or whatever you could call it, and without it, he realised immediately, he was alone. Now he was free, if you could call this sense of loneliness freedom. If only he had the courage to get out. If only he had the nerve to go and find himself. Then he thought that there's nothing to find. Anyway, there was Victoria to think about. How would she respond to his absence? Of course, she didn't actually need him. She had so many other calls on her time, yet she'd always been the one he turned to. She had always been there. Maybe he was just a nuisance, something she was anchored to. The kids would miss him for a bit, perhaps, but they didn't need him either. Face it, I'm all washed up, written out, guilt-strewn, and directionless.

And yet. Look at the girl swaying unhappily on the seat in front of him. He'd noticed her. He hadn't been too inward-looking to notice her. He wasn't completely lost if he could notice her. She really was lovely. As a passing thought, he allowed himself to imagine how satisfying it would be if she allowed him to comfort her about whatever trouble she found herself. See, he told himself, he was not an emotional desert after all. There could still be dreams.

They stopped again. This time, the young musician jumped to her feet straight away, stumbling past him in her rush to the doors. He inhaled her soap smell above the sweat-filled carriage as she passed. Then she was gone. He watched her walk away, fading out of his life as the train picked up speed again.

Victoria

Victoria Kassoloniki–Bicky, as everyone here seemed to call her —suffered the low hum of the city all around her as she drove home. She wished that her husband would be there waiting for her. She wanted someone to talk to about tomorrow's programme; she wished he'd listened to today's, but as far as she knew, San Miguel de las Colinas, still less Artemio's Fire, was outside the range of their capital transmitters.

She sighed with frustration as she turned to drive through the gate. Maria had come out to open it for her when she had sounded the horn. She checked the clock on the dashboard. She was only ten minutes late. The traffic on the Avenida de los Revolucionarios had been worse than she had anticipated. At least it looked as if she had gotten here before that rat of a husband Maria was lumbered to, poor woman. He wasn't hanging around in his taxi waiting for her. He, too, had probably been held up. He'd be here soon, though. He'd pick up his wife, take her home and, Bicky thought angrily, spots of colour suddenly appearing on her alabaster cheeks, beat the shit out of her.

The man was unspeakable. How did Maria stand for it? She would never put up with such a situation. She would not have stayed after the first slap or punch if she had been in the maid's shoes. My

24

God, if Alex ever did something like that to her. But he wouldn't. He loved her. He was big, and reedy, gentle and aloof. When he stood beside her at one of those interminable parties given by some institution or embassy, she felt his protection cloak her with energy. When he was at home and she stroked the thick beard he had always worn, now increasingly flecked with grey, she felt wanted and safe.

It would have been nicer if Martin had liked him better, and of course, she wished that her father had been able to give his blessing to their union. But she couldn't have everything. The three men she had loved most in her life all loved her, it seemed, without question. That was not something to be taken lightly, even if two of them couldn't or didn't particularly like each other.

Martin was not alone in the unease he felt when Alex was around. Most people found Victoria's husband strange, with his tall gangly stoop and that faraway look in his foreign eyes as he hovered over his wife. He was protective but somehow absent, his gaze fixed far away on some dream of a mountain, a rage of magma blasting across his reverential vision.

That was one of the reasons she loved him, of course. His unreachability made him mysterious to her, a protean figure, a robed Merlin only temporarily attached to earth. Yet when he gave his whole attention to the here and now of her, she was lit up in flames, even after a double wrench of childbirth, and despite the cares of parenting and ownership. When Alex was really with her she spent the whole time seething with anticipation, tectonically precarious and alive. Then, far too early, he would be gone again, off on another quest, and she would not believe, with any certainty, that he would ever come back.

Perhaps I love him so much because of how I first saw him, she sometimes told herself. Perhaps all first moments colour what happens after. If you get off to a good start, you stand a chance of making it work. If the beginning is grubby or ordinary, then you can probably look forward to a messy lifetime of squabble and awkward separations. But, if the first time you see your lover, he is silhouetted against the setting sun high up on ruined castle walls atop a hill, sniffing the aromatic woodsmoke on the evening air, then the first sight of that tall beanpole of a bearded mystic questing out the magic of distant lands will affect all your subsequent judgements. She had always thought that it would take a lot to turn such a man into something ordinary.

Martin thought he was crazy straight away. But Martin had been difficult ever since they had started out on their adventure all those years ago. Given the circumstances, they could not have done anything else. Their grandmother, who was almost as shocked as they were, was vehemently against their departure. She was not alone in her disagreement with the young siblings' wanderings. The other grandparents (distant and disapproving from across the water), two aunts, the neighbours, and friends of the family all felt that Victoria and Martin were doing something wrong. The natural order had already been violated. Why must they add to the sense of dislocation? Only their disreputable uncle, roused by an indignant sister from his contemplation of ruin at the bottom of an oily glass seemed to approve of what they had decided. Let them roam. Let them find themselves, he intoned with exaggerated seriousness, each word enunciated with great care to disguise the state he was in. They need time. They have the rest of their lives to try and get used to now. Give them their heads, give them some sort of freedom, not your censure.

In truth, none of the adults around them really knew what to do about the young brother and sister, so suddenly abandoned. They all had grief to cope with, too. They all had to accommodate feelings of guilt and rage and face this sudden reminder of their own precariousness. Of course, they would never do anything so incalculably selfish themselves. It was against all nature. It offended everything they all thought they believed in. But death is death and despair was something most people know about after their youth has gone.

"Poor buggers," Victoria's disreputable uncle said, referring to his brother and sister-in-law. "Poor children," the others said, referring to Vicky and Martin, wondering how great was the damage they had suffered.

Maybe Martin saw an echo of his own father's cadaverous last stares in the gaunt stranger perched above the aromatic valley, Vicky thought that day. Maybe he was instinctively frightened of the possibility of her loving someone else. After all, they had both seen what love, cursed love, could do, and yes, it might be perfectly understandable. But in the end, she and her brother had been permanently excluded. Anyway, up until now this whole trip had been dominated by loss for both of them. They were adrift in an alien environment since it, the unmentionable thing, had happened.

Martin, the brother who had once been only familiar, was now his whole family. As the oldest of the two, she felt responsible for both of them. She was sure he had resented the awkward stranger who might take her away. At least that's the way she saw it, Victoria told herself when she looked back upon that day and the days which followed. That's what I imagine Martin was feeling. Poor Martin.

They had got so much more used to each other over the last twenty-odd years since then. There was a proud interdependence where once there had been only pain. Now they could say that they had made it through this far, despite everything that had happened. Or, they would have done. But as if it was not bad enough losing their parents like that, her poor brother had to go through it again when Margarita died. He had lost, all those years ago, the people he depended upon, and now he was free of the one person (a sister-substitute? Victoria wondered again) who had depended on him.

All this was to come on that evening when she first saw her future husband. Martin, being bad-tempered as he had been for the last week, was complaining about the climbing. Earlier that day, he had said without thinking that he was fed up with all this travelling around. He hated going from one ruin to another, trying to imagine past battles in modern clay. All he wanted to do was go home. His eyes had watered as he realised what that meant, and he had been angry ever since because he knew that Victoria had seen.

She had not been mature enough at the time to say that they each had to find their way of dealing with the fact that their own mother, who their father loved so much and who was besotted with him in return, had blown her husband's head off with his old rabbit-shooter. Then she put the barrel between her own lovely lips to blast bloodied accretions of brain marrow and skull shards all over the walls and the ceiling behind her. They might have under-

27

stood the fact that she had put their father out of his terminal misery, but even now, when Victoria thought she knew what real love between two consenting adults felt like, she could not understand how her own mother, who might still be a friend, could have preferred oblivion to the healthy love that a woman should have for her own children.

You do what you can to deal with things. That's what she should have told her brother back then. I am filling my head, she might have said, with ancient tales of bravery and treachery, of sacrifice and heroism. The dark spaces in my mind have been blocked out by visions of bearded heroes, bronze-limbed and naked in all their mysterious beauty, clutching spears and shields as they marched into battle. It even felt, as she looked down the steep hill and out over the valley, that she could almost hear their cries on the evening air.

And it was at this very moment that she saw Alexei Kassoniliki contemplating the titanic mystery of this fragile earth. She knew, instinctively, that he could replace any fantasy she might otherwise have to rely on. She was suddenly deliriously hopeful.

What if they had not gone up to that castle all those years ago, she caught herself thinking as she watched Maria close the gates behind her. She would not be here. There would be no children—well, not these children, anyway. God only knows where Martin would be. She watched her maid in the mirror. If she hadn't met Alex then, she thought, she would not even know that a stout dependable woman who was not by any means stupid had to undergo the relentless humiliation of being hit by an ignorant bully of a husband. Such chance meetings ripple out along the tracks of their lives and soon they cannot imagine how it could have been otherwise.

She got out of the car, pulling her briefcase after her. The alarm screeched as she pressed the remote control tag on her key ring. She turned back to Maria. "I'm sorry I'm late," she said to the maid. "The traffic was bad on the Avenida de los Revolucionarios. I got here as soon as I could."

"There is no reason to preoccupy yourself, Señora," Maria said. "The children are watching television, and my husband is not yet here himself. No doubt he is struck in traffic, too."

Angelita

Angelita Hernandez Remedios immediately noticed the staring gringo on the metro. He was so obvious, after all. She'd seen someone else looking at her as she came out of the station, too. But none of them, on or off the train, had made much impression upon her. She was looking inwards and backwards, not outwards.

It was the professor's attitude towards her after it had happened back there in his office, as he struggled to clothe himself, that had shown her, with a sudden clarity, that she had fallen for the oldest falsehood in a young woman's psyche. She had succumbed to the most obvious wiles of an older man's self-delusion. Stripped of what she had thought of as love, and once the bodily urge had so quickly evaporated, her teacher had looked as if he might be her father. The thought of her committing to him like that was now ridiculous.

His brilliance, manifested in the sharp glint of his eye—even the magic of his bow across the strings, was punctured by the reality of his flabby nakedness and his pusillanimity in the face of the spotty boy who stood there open-mouthed and inane. Yet all of this might not have mattered so much if Jacinto Perez, the great and frightening maestro, had just once, by a look of understanding or even a plea for help, acknowledged her complicity. Then she might not have felt so exposed. But from the moment the door had opened

29

and he had drawn himself clumsily away from her, she seemed to have ceased to exist. When he had once looked at her, she had seen only apparent indifference in his face, and thought it cruelly truthful because it was obviously entirely unintentional.

For the moment, it was too early to wonder whether she would go on having lessons with her seducer—she grimaced at the thought —or whether she would stay on at the *conservatorio* at all. Right now, all she could think of, over and over again, was that she had been a fool, and that she had been made a fool of. She had done something stupid and wrong.

She comforted herself with the assumption that the professor would never tell anyone about it, and that she was hardly going to broadcast her own part in the escapade, but the scene with the boy was highly ambiguous. All he had said when she had struggled into her clothes and tried to say goodbye, was "my son." Perhaps there would be some huge scene—the boy looked crazy enough. Perhaps the professor's wife would get hysterical and tell the world about her husband and the… She could almost feel the public shame already. If it got too much for her, she might end up blabbing herself. She'd probably have to tell her friend Julio. What a mess she had got herself into.

A drunk, probably one of the many homeless who inhabited the city streets, lay slumped in the doorway of the block of flats where she lived. His greasy hair leaked out from a threadbare cap. He was protected from the weather by something that might once have been a sleeping bag. The smell of old Blanquita, acid and stale, rose to her nostrils, and she stepped over the unconscious man with a guilty distaste.

It wasn't yet dark, and he was already *borrachisimo*, completely drunk. Yet that's not it, she knew, as she put her key into the outer door. People don't choose to live like that. It happens to them. People don't choose to lose their wives or husbands either. But it had happened to her father. That's why she was not allowed to mention her mother's name at home. That's why, of all people, her father must not know that his little angel had got herself into a compromising position with a man almost his same age. And, what was worse, a man who had a wife. Federico Hernandez Placencia was, after all, that rarest of beings, a genuinely moral man, desperately trying to keep his own integrity together in the unkind world of politics and struggle.

Angelita loved her father unquestioningly and, even more, she respected him. His eccentricities amused her; his dedication filled her with awe. When he told her off or did something she did not like, she assumed it was her fault. When she didn't want to tell him her secrets, she enjoyed the subterfuges she employed to stop him from being hurt or concerned. Like him, she was headstrong and, sometimes willful. She pursued her own goals with the same rigour as he fought his causes, working at how best to win him round when he disapproved of some action of hers. Over the last few years, they had fought many battles, but they had been conflicts of love. They both knew how and when, in the end, to give in. Her father's happiness was a joy to her; his approval was the one thing she craved.

When she walked through the front door of the flat, as she did now, and heard his gruff ¡*Hola mi Angelita!* (as she did now as well), she would feel safe and whole. She would be restored by the smell of their home, a mix of cooking and cigarette smoke, her father's aftershave, floor polish, and the city's pungent exhalations seeping in through the open windows. But this time, a shudder passed through her. She wondered if her face would give any hint of what had happened earlier in the day. Perhaps there were some terrible marks on her neck or on her clothes. She was suddenly overwhelmed by an attack of self-consciousness.

She put her violin case down in the hall and laid her music case against it. "I'll be with you in a minute, Papa," she called out, and dived into the bathroom before he could call to her in reply.

Federico Hernandez Placencia sat in the room which, ever since his wife's desertion, he had used as a second office, a place to wage his campaigns and for setting the world to rights in. As he sifted papers, the lazily spiralling smoke from the cigarette he had absentmindedly abandoned in the ashtray to his right suddenly changed course on an almost imperceptible breath of air. He felt the smoke's dance and reached for its source in a reflexive action. As he drew the fresh exhaust deep into his lungs, intoxicated by the nicotine hit it gave him, he went back to reading the report that had come in the

31

morning's post. It was about a week too late, but it was still interesting, if deeply worrying.

Federico was a firm believer in organised, peaceful protest, seeing it as a bedrock of democracy. Yet, what he understood about the group of *compañeros* down south he was reading about sounded more like anarchy with a potentially violent undertow. That couldn't be right. The only way to convince this government, any government they had, and to win over the people if it came to that, was by peaceful mass protest, a powerful witness to injustice, a measured call for the improvement of working people's lives. This improvement would surely come about, he had always believed, when the overwhelming mass of the population joined their cause, moved by their dogged decency.

His old father had recently told him, for example, about a group of white-hooded protesters fighting the injustice of the five *casiques* beyond the valley of San Miguel. That interested him. It seemed the right thing to do because, according to his father, some ordinary Migueleños were impressed by their peaceful behaviour and calm logic. That's how you won people over to your side. But, no one would ever get involved if they were frightened off by careless violence.

Son of a bitch, this country had seen enough of that in his father's and grandfather's days: the massacre of innocents, brother against brother, or one side of a street hating people only a few metres away on the other. There were still a few older people around who could remember the revolution firsthand. It had promised so much and, if you thought about it cynically, had achieved so little. There had been the creation of a particular kind of national pride, it was true, with all the myths of heroism and sacrifice. But, the rich were still getting richer, workers were still being exploited, and as for the government, everyone knew they were all on the take with their *mordidas* here, the suborning of contracts there. On bad days, it was profoundly depressing. You had to try to do something about it, otherwise, you became old and cynical—like they were.

It must not be imagined that Federico hated his country or its history. On the contrary, he loved it with a fierce possessiveness. He gloried in its heroes and heroines: the young men who had lost their lives in principled revolt against abusive landowners, the women who had harboured them and, revolutionary lore insisted, fought alongside them even as they loved them and conceived their children. Those were the people he idolised and whose music his heart hummed along with. Of course, they had achieved some things. A tyrant had been overthrown, a sort of justice had prevailed for a time, the chaining of labourers to the rich man's land had been largely discontinued as a result, and some of the laws looked much better when it was all over than when it had begun. Except you could get round any laws in this country if you had the money.

Federico had learned to talk up justice ever since he had been a little boy. His parents' house, built on a hilltop overlooking the town of San Miguel de las Colinas, always seemed to be full of people plotting and planning late into the night. His father was at the centre of these discussions, his thick moustache quivering and his dark eyes widening into luminous circles. His thick black brows arched with concentrated passion above his angular cheekbones. His prominent nose was just modest enough not to be considered long. He made a handsome figure. For young Federico he was everything he thought a man ought to be as he rode up the hillside to their flat-roofed home built round a central courtyard, modest in scope with its bare adobe walls, but noisy and occupied.

Don Esteban would spur the horse through the arched entry before forcing it to a sudden halt in front of the trough which stood against the back wall by the kitchen area and food store. Once there, the ranchero would swing a long leg up and over the pommel of the saddle, leap off his panting mount, and loosen the heaving girth before the startled animal had time to lurch forward and plunge its greedy mouth into the water. Then, the careless man would turn away and stride into the kitchen, pushing his sweat-brimmed hat back off his head. Federico loved the deep ridge furrowed into his father's forehead which would be thus exposed, and would watch him with awe as he plunged a ladle into the pitcher of iced juice. His mother had prepared it for her husband and he tipped the refreshing liquid down his undulating throat.

His father was old now, his thick black hair transformed into a sparse netting of grey tendrils, his strong cheekbones hangers for the drapes of flesh which folded thinly down towards the crosshatch lines around his mouth. The widowed patriarch did not approve of his son and the choices he had made, and it seemed to Federico that there were issues they still had to resolve. Yet, the old man's welcome seemed genuine on the occasions when he made the journey out of the city to see him as he hovered in the decaying house with Tia Rosario and her simple-minded daughter.

What really made the old man happy were the visits of his beloved Angelita, Federico's only child. She had a fragile beauty almost too perfect to comprehend (the old man had said) and a smile of such enigmatic welcome that even now he told his son that his life had not been lived in vain. *"Angelita de mi corazon,"* he would wheeze as she came through the crumbling arch, smiling at the tang of hilly air, so different from the city stew she lived in. "You are here," her grandfather would gloat. "You should come more often." But when she charmed him out of his old man's querulousness, and Federico saw the adoration the old man's eyes, it made him inordinately proud even as it made him savagely jealous. He allowed himself, in his less sensible moments, to think it was unfair that it should be her that Don Esteban loved and not him.

But back then, standing on the roof as the sun sank behind the hills, looking down at the town, across the valley to where the volcano, their own new volcano, smoked lazily in the dusk, his father would put a heavy muscled arm across his boyish shoulders and tell him tales of revolution. All this, he would say expansively, taking in their house and beyond it to where he and his brother raised their beef cattle, is because of the revolution, because of your grandfather who died for justice, he and his *compañeros*. It is all that we have was fought for. Once we were landless peasants—now all that has changed. You must never forget this lesson, *hijo mio*. Swear you will never forget. The boy looked up at his father's blazing eyes and make his vows with enthusiasm.

At other times, the Don would fix him with a serious stare. There is still so much to do, *mi hijo*, he would worry, gazing out over the breakfast table. Later on, when he was older, as they watched the cattle plodding gingerly through the scrubby grass, he would say,

"We won back much of our land. We stopped the slavery of the old beholden ones. Hell, we even got rid of that old bastard president with his cruelty and corruption. But you have to watch these *cabrones*, understand? If we don't keep an eye on them." He grasped his son by his shoulders and faced him down so that the boy felt the power of his smoky breath. "They'll screw us all over again."

He was doing his best, Federico told himself. He was a father, too, and about the same age as his own had been at about the time of their big argument. What more could he do, he kept asking himself. His father should be pleased with him, his son. He should have been pleased with him even then. He should have seen what he would do. Jesus Maria, he knew how to fight for his clients and he keeps doing it, on and on, even though the battle is hard and the war is long and he suffered many defeats. But how could he fight for his Angelita? Damn music (he smiled to himself, hearing his own father's recriminations). Why did she have to do that?

He heard the bathroom door open and listened for her footsteps along the corridor. When she came into the room he waited a second or two before he looked up at her, postponing the moment. When he did see her, he gasped. Her face was washed clean of the city dirt, her thick black hair, freshly brushed and combed, was pulled severely back from her wide forehead. She smiled at him, but her impeccable eyes were edgy, troubled beneath the carapace of love she wore for him. She looks so beautiful he thought, so vulnerable. What was he to do with her? How could he love her? How could he protect her?

"Hello, Papa," she said, coming over to kiss him on the forehead. "Have you had a good day?"

He marvelled at the whisper of her face as he always did. "Yes," he replied. "I think I may have got the cement workers out of their predicament. I think." He told her these things because there was no one else there to tell, even though he knew she was not really interested. "What about you, child? All that music? What is it all for?"

This was a familiar routine. He thought he knew what she would say. He was surprised when, for once, she did not come back with her usual rejoinder.

"What is music for?" she asked instead, her voice low and worried, becoming more animated as she talked. "It is about life. It is about the thoughts I have, the thoughts you have. It is about a place we can all go to receive comfort and love and pain. When I play well, that is if I play well—I can play well Papa, honestly I can." (As if he ever doubted it.) "I know that the world is good, that there is some point to it all, to what we are and what we do. When I play the world goes away. It is the best thing I can do. At least I thought it was until..." Her voice faded to silence in a breathless diminuendo.

When Angelita looked down at her father, worried that she had said too much, she saw the concern on his face. She felt comforted and irritated by it at the same time. She sat down in the tattered armchair. There was no sound in the room. They sat in a listless silence, each with their own thoughts and preoccupations. The girl wondered how she was going to live down this feeling of shame and discomfort. Federico wondered what it was about the world that Angelita should wish it away.

Maria

Maria could not stand it anymore. They had been stuck in this traffic jam, a great perspiring cacophony of vehicles, for half an hour. All around them engines rattled and murmured in the heavy air, a thousand million particles of burnt fuel rising ominously into the evening atmosphere.

Juan kept trying to make conversation. She found this irritating. "I had a good day," he said. "You should be pleased. I made the double of what I normally bring home." When she failed to answer, he started to whistle tunelessly. Then, after a few minutes in which his whistling echoed uncomfortably in the relative silence of the car's interior, he shouted abuse at a pedestrian weaving through the nearly stationary traffic. Then he tuned the radio to a station playing loud brassy hits from some earlier decade.

They moved forward in badly syncopated hops and skips. Juan reached forward and turned the music down. "Traffic's bad today," he said. "My God, it was backed up all the way to the Ancestor Monument. You don't get that very often. I reckon it was the football match. What do you think?"

All Maria could think was that her husband's gregarious cheerfulness was monumentally unfair. His attempts to talk normally to her were gross violations of her resentful solitude. How could he behave like this after last night? Then he had bridled when she asked him for some extra money to fix the battered old washing machine. She depended on it because she really didn't want to wash their clothes by hand after a hard day at the house of Señora Bicky.

"I'm not made of money," he growled at her.

She replied quietly that she knew that, but she worked as hard as she could already.

"What?" he had said. "I suppose you think you're something special skivvying around for some rich *gringa*. Well, let me tell you what I have to put up with out there on those shitty streets day after day. That's work, you stupid cow, not the unimportant little jobs that you do in that big house. Cleaning. Jesus."

"Then how come you don't bring back enough money if you work so hard?" she whispered under her breath, as if thinking to her herself.

"What?" he hissed, his eyes narrowing dangerously so that she thought, *Oh no, dear God, Mary mother of God, not again. What's the matter with me? Why can't I keep my big mouth shut?*

"Nothing," she said. "Nothing important, *mi amor.*"

"Don't you '*mi amor*' me, woman. What did you say?"

"Just that I, well, that I need more money."

"Money? Money? You want more money? Is that all you ever think of? Jesus Christ, is that all you ever ever think of?"

She said nothing then, hoping it would pass. Sometimes it did.

"Well? he insisted, is that all you think of?" He grabbed her by the arm, his fingers sinking heavily into her skin, raising indented hillsides in the flab of her muscles. "Is it?" he shouted.

She knew now that he was working himself up, getting ready to strike her.

Still, after all these years, she had no idea of how to behave. She had no way of preventing the beating which would surely follow his increasing anger. Each time she thought he might relax under the influence of her obvious pleading, which was the only response she was capable of. Each time she knew he would not, and was thus conscious again of her own failure. It was all her fault.

"Please, my husband, please *mi amor*," she implored him quietly, her head bowed submissively. "You are hurting my arm. It hurts. Please let me go."

"You're hurting my arm!" he mimicked cruelly. "You're hurting my arm. You stupid bitch. That's not hurting. You want to know what hurting feels like? This is what hurting fucking feels like."

Like the driver skidding unstoppably towards the head-on impact, she felt no fear in that moment. She saw his arm raised and watched it stretch out towards her, frame by frame, the weight of the shoulder, the curve of the elbow, the flexing wrist, the bunched knuckles and joints. For a second, slowed and isolated in the unreality of her heightened alarm, she thought, *I could dodge the blow this time.* She almost smiled at her herself for this perception. But then, she felt his fist slam into her cheek bone, and her head jerked violently to one side. She felt a crunch of enamel as she bit into the edges of her tongue, and her eyes shut automatically at the impact.

She heard the roaring in her head first, and then the pain started, not gradually, but in an instant cymbal crash of agony.

"¡Ay! ¡Ay! ¡Ay!" She pulled away from him and though she knew it was the worst thing to do, she started to cry.

He hit her twice more screaming, "Don't fucking cry, woman, Christ, the slightest bloody problem and you start wailing like that. Stop it for God's sake. I can't stand you bloody blubbering."

And he hit her again.

Then, as so often, he suddenly stopped, deflated and shrunken, his passion spent, the shame hovering above him, waiting to fill the void left by his departing anger. She half observed this through the part of her brain that was not overwhelmed with horror, with the cacophony of bruised outrage that echoed through her and around her. There was a whirling dizziness in her head. She thought she was going to throw up. She was poisoned by a terrible, sick, familiar complicity, working out the ways that this was all her doing.

Juan went out shortly after that, unable, she thought, to bear her sulky pain. He was also unwilling to accept responsibility for the marks on her cheek that were already turning into bruises. After he left, she sat and snivelled, her mind blank with depression. The pain walled her in. She turned off the lights and sat in a mirror-free darkness punctuated only by the orange glow of the city at night. She hardly dare make a sound in case Doña Esmeralda heard her from next door. She'd have to come in and pour the poison of her sympathy into Maria's open wounds.

She was asleep when he returned, safe in her unconsciousness. She woke when he tried to embrace her, clumsily suggesting an act of love to heal their injuries. But he was too ashamed or too drunk to insist when she parried his encircling arms with her own disgusted lack of co-operation.

In the morning, he avoided her eyes and complained of a hangover as if she were sympathetic. He completed her conversation turns for her when she failed to respond like a mother would with her baby. When he said goodbye to her on Señora Bicky's street, he took his leave of her with apparent geniality. Now, at the end of a long day's housework and childcare, here he was as they headed home in the stinking traffic, pretending to be cheerful again, chatting to her as normal husbands might do, and it hurt her even more than the rasp of her bruises or the dull ache which encircled her skull.

The damn city was to blame, Juan was telling himself as he chattered on, trying to get things back to where they had once been. If she could just stop judging him the whole time, they could have a conversation as if from the beginning. He glanced at her as she sat silent and threatening beside him. No chance of that. It's the city, then, that's what the problem is, the great obscene hungry guts of this city.

Sometimes the smog was so thick you could hardly breathe. He'd peer through his cracked windshield, and through the ugly grey spawn of it, he would only be able to see for a couple blocks. Then the traffic would grind to a halt and the klaxons would sound. Cars to the side and behind him would start their febrile jockeying for position. He'd feel the people on the seat behind him begin to panic as they realised they were going to be late for whatever it was he was taking them to. Holy Mother of God, it was more than an ordinary man should be asked to bear.

It was, in a way, Maria's fault that they were here. Fifteen years ago, she was the one who'd suggested they move here to their cramped little apartment hung on a hillside. It was well within the

40

smog zone where the electricity supply was unreliable, and the smell of clogged drains hovered in the evening air. Well, it might have been her. But anyway, if he'd known, he'd never have agreed to come. They could have stayed back in the village, kept a cow, maybe two, and forced their mules to pull a plough through the sterile earth. Oh God, for a breath of country air. Then he thought of what she would say, what his wretched wife would say now if he accused her.

You're forgetting how dry it was, she'd moan at him, *how bored we were. We had no money. We were dirt poor. That's why we came here.* She would go on about the dusty topsoil which stung their skin in the hot wind and the relentless diet of beans and pancakes leavened only by the slaughter of some anorexic pig on occasional feast days. Their diet had marked them, cracked his plainsman's teeth and stopped their bodies' luxurious development.

It had always been assumed that he would marry Maria. They were neighbours. The families expected it. And so, at the appropriate age they had been joined together by the old priest in the bare chapel which stood tucked under the hillside at the end of their valley. Then they had set about doing what couples do together, but apart from one early still-born child, there had been no others. Their lives were as dry as the powdery dirt around them. The idea of the city had seemed the right escape. A new and exciting life—bright lights, more money, more love.

That dream had not lasted long. Now they were snagged on the money they owed for rent and the loan he had taken out on the taxi. He could have paid it back if he hadn't lost so much on racing. "All our savings?" Maria had screamed, incredulous, before he hit her. That had been two years ago. Now they were pretty much back where they started, and try as they might, with him working all the hours God sent and his wife slaving away for the foreign family, they were trapped. And for what?

A large truck belching smoke moved past them on Maria's side of the car. Just as it drew even with them, the driver pulled the string above his head. To the tractor roar in her ears was added the trumpeting of the air horns mounted on either side of the cab. That did it. Something very much like the pain of a man's fist exploded again in her head. Something very much like a woman grievously wronged exploded in her breast, and with a cry and an obscenity that no one would ever have imagined her making use of, she threw open the door and got out of the car.

For a moment she looked around her, confused by what she had done and what she should do next. All she was conscious of was the hot vapour of burnt gas and the neutral stare of a thousand lidded windscreens. She did not know where to go. She heard Juan shouting at her through the open window that had, until a second ago, been hers.

"Maria, woman, what the hell do you think you're doing?" But it was a voice that didn't interest her. She could not understand the words. All she knew, she said later, was that she wanted to get away and so she started walking back the way they had come, making her way between the lines of traffic as if unaware of her own vulnerability.

At first, Juan did not know what to do. His wife's actions were so surprising that he had no way of understanding them. When he came partly to his senses he jumped out of the taxi, too. Leaping quickly between two cars, he ran to catch up with her. Grabbing her bruised arm, he spun her round to face him.

"What in the name of all the saints are you thinking of?" he demanded, his voice unsteady with the drama of it all.

"Let go of me!" she screamed.

He could just hear her voice above the engine rumble all around them. Something in that voice was so unexpected that he did as she commanded. She turned and walked away again, leaving him standing there, humiliated in front of all those people.

"Hey!" he shouted, running after her again. "What the fuck's going on? Have you lost your head? Are you trying to make a fool of me?" This time he ran ahead of her so that he stood in front of her, blocking her progress, his arms bunched at his side. Maria didn't answer, nor did she look at him. Her gaze passed over his shoulder, as if he was invisible.

"Silly bitch!" he screamed, grabbing the hair on her neck and forcing her head backwards. "Have you gone nuts or what the fuck?"

The first horns started then. Beyond his wife's head, Juan could see that the cars stretching in front of his stationary taxi had started to move.

"Come on," he said, releasing her hair and grabbing her by the wrist, "we've got to move. Stop all this foolishness, come on."

He tried to pull her back to the taxi but again, in that frightening voice, she just said, "Let me go."

He nearly did. But more car horns were sounding now, voices were raised in anger, and the lanes of traffic on either side of his started to move, too.

Juan looked around him desperately as if there might be someone there to help him. But his private drama hardly interested the frustrated inhabitants of all the vehicles around him. The klaxons had built into a devilish scherzo, angry and shocking.

"Come on," shouted a voice. "Sort it out in your own time. Get back in your car!"

"Give her a good slap," yelled someone else, "and get out of here."

"What's the matter?" mocked a passing truck driver. "Can't control your woman? Stupid bastard!"

"Please!" Juan yelled at his wife, diminished and afraid, his panic increasing as the pressure mounted. "Please Maria, please!"

She just prised his fingers, one by one, from her wrist and walked past him and away.

The taxi driver had no choice in the end. The whole city seemed to be honking and screaming at him. He had to run back to his cab and move. He had to. Anything else would have been unpardonable. He drove away with tears of shame bubbling from somewhere deep inside him. *Shit. God damn it. Why?*

He was unable to get to the side of the avenue because of the regimented lines of metal on either side of him. In his rearview mirror, he saw her disappearing behind him, a frail stranger in his sudden nightmare. When he was finally able to make his way across the rows of cars and trucks and double back to look for her, she was nowhere to be seen.

It was dark when Maria got back to Señora Bicky's house. Her feet hurt from all the walking, her chest hurt from the poison of the

43

city's arteries, and her eyes were stinging from the assault of all that dust.

She did not really know why she had come to this sloped street, with its elegant homes relaxing back behind carefully maintained verges and barriers against unwanted entry. But it was, at least, a place he never came to, even when he dropped her here for work or came to pick her up at the end of the day. Perhaps this house she spent so much time in, far from the reach of his intemperate arms, could be a place of safety. She was due back here in not too many hours anyway, so it made a certain sense.

She rang the bell and watched to see the light in the hall switched on. The door opened, and her employer stood in the entrance peering out towards the gate.

"Who is it?" Vicky Kassoliniki called.

Maria tried to say, "Señora, it's me, *Maria a sus ordenes*," but her voice made no sound. By the time Vicky had come out of the house, and realised who stood there, she opened the gate. The maidservant was mute and immobile. Her face was canyoned with the overflow of her tears.

Jacinto

WHAT DO you say to an insecure teenager when he has seen his father doing *that* with someone who was clearly not his mother? That would, of course, be bad enough; as a committed sensualist, Professor Jacinto Perez was perfectly aware of the irredeemable awfulness of contemplating one's own parents sweating and grunting together in a way that youth regards as intensely private, and which they assume, belongs to them alone. Yet this was significantly more serious than a son's knowledge of a father's legitimate carnality; not only was retribution from his wife an obvious possibility but the boy's own mental state was something that preoccupied the violinist greatly.

It was all so unfamiliar. He was used to the fleeting guilt he felt every time he broke that old oath. But then, it always seemed so innocent and nothing less than he deserved—he who laboured to make the world more beautiful by his art. He had never really contemplated any consequences of true discovery. He had even taken a curious kind of paternal excitement from one girl he'd been obliged to help with her 'problem'. He had been gratified when she had told him, bleakly, that it had been the right thing to do and that he had been so wise in the way he had supported her. He accepted her praise. He thought of that girl, all of them, as his protégées, and used his extraordinary memory to sweeten out, in his own mind, the hollowness of their encounters once it was over. Instead he recollected, with pride, their sexy flirtations—the way a garment had fallen to the floor, the manner in which they had held him, the rings they wore, or the brush of their eyelashes.

Now, however, sitting at the dinner table on the twenty-third floor of their apartment block with the stinking city laid out like glittering jewels of refracted light as far as the eye could see, the revered teacher and renowned virtuoso had no idea what to say. Even after his wife, the once famous soprano Marisa Sepulveda de Perez, had sent the maid away, he could find no words. He simply could not summon the jocularity with which he usually tried to oil the machinery of family discourse.

He looked over at his wife, watching the heavy jowls rise and fall, the skin fluttering loosely with every determined mastication of her powerful jaws. Guiltily, from above his half-moon glasses, he studied the made-up lips in her middle-aged face, the buried lines and contours of the appearance which, when he had first encountered it twenty-five years ago on his most successful foreign trip, had filled him with awe. He was playing two of the world's favourite concertos. She was singing songs on the death of children and arias of jubilation. When he had seen her sweet smile, the luxurious shape beneath the absurdly crenolated folds and stiff stays which women on the concert platform seemed to be obliged to wear, he was suddenly lost with a lurch of physical desire which filled his underwear with longing and made him want to cry out. And she, like so many others before and since, had been entranced by his feline haughtiness. She had been overcome by the majesty of his playing as his arms pulled cascades of unimaginably beautiful scales and arpeggios from his willing fiddle, long sinuous lines of ascending melody held in the air by his extraordinary technique.

They were, in fact, overwhelmed by each other's artistry at the same moment as they were aware of each other's physicality. When he came off the stage one night, in one of the world's great capitals, with the bravos ringing in his ears and the tears of gratitude dotting the faces of his audience, she was waiting for him outside her dressing room. He had only to say one simple word, *Marisa*, before they had shut the door on the imploring crowds and bolted it shut. Then he had cast his seventeenth-century violin of great worth to one side and they had plunged into each other with an excess of fortissimo ardour, an incandescent abandon which had shocked them both with its fierce glory. When, half an hour later, the concert organiser hammered on her door, desperate for her post-interval appearance on the stage, the violinist was slumped in a corner, emptied out, experiencing half-sleeping hallucinations of profound perfection and previously unimagined perversions.

But, the great singer, her eyes almost popping out of her head, let her voluminous dress fall back down over her exquisite thighs, still rippling with great muscular convulsions after the roar of joy they had managed to create, and marched from the room, out before her waiting public, still feeling as if her body would melt beneath her, to give a performance of such heart-stopping tenderness that at the end the conductor was able to hold his baton awkwardly aloft for more than a minute while the audience held their breath in mute appreciation. There was not a cough, not a shifted buttock, no surreptitious watch glance, and afterwards, when they were allowed to, they wept and the applause was difficult, almost sacrilegious, because they all knew that music of such great interpretation, so poignant, so visceral, was more than humankind could bear, even though it was what made sense of their lives.

The violinist and the soprano tried again and again to recreate the extraordinary fact of that fateful interval. They promised love. They sang and played for each other, shared concerts around the globe, made music, naked, in the tropics and reached for each other's secret places beneath heavy covers in the great coldnesses of the north. Though they coupled ceaselessly, frontwards and backwards, generous with all their orifices, considerate of each other's timings and lusts, the eruption of joy they had once experienced always seemed to exist just outside their grasping reach. They experimented in all the known ways of love from the hedonistic manuals of the present to eastern collections of historical mysticism and profound eroticism. Even though they used each other in ways they had never before contemplated, they never again achieved the ecstatic union of their first unbridled intercourse.

It must be like music, Jacinto told himself, where the most heart-stopping performance is only available in any real form as it hangs in the excited air around you. "There are no recordings of music like that," he would tell his pupils. "No regurgitated music will ever penetrate your brain like that." When the music has climaxed, he might have added, and the soloist holds his detumescent instrument carelessly by his side to receive the plaudits of the crowd, why then it has all gone and its translucent presence in our memory is all that is left to feed dreams of unrealistic perfection forever.

So the love between the singer and the violinist gradually cooled, and Jacinto Perez began to realise what a strange contract he had made. This wasn't just because Marisa's mother, an almost witch-like figure, insisted on staying in the menial job she had worked at for years even though her daughter was now wealthy enough to give her unimaginable comforts. It wasn't just the old woman's quirky mysticism and her local fame as a medium. It was something else, too—an echo of the mother's craziness in her daughter's increasing periods of silence from which he was shut out. It was a knowledge that Marisa was quite capable of inhabiting some world of spirits that he knew absolutely nothing about. When he had tried to ask her about it, she rebuffed him and told him not to be so stupid, and so, gradually he stopped asking. Over the years, he convinced himself that he had been mistaken, and that Marisa, far from being mad, was just that kind of a wife.

By the time he knew every nook and cranny of his opera-singing lover—the mole on her inner thigh just there by the hair-line, the blemish by her left nipple, and the muscle kink in her haunch—he realised that, for him at least, the magic had gone, and that she was pregnant. They got married, and her breasts leaked milk while he began his lifelong contemplation of ecstasy denied.

She stopped singing when the twins were born. "I'll resume my career," she said, "when they are older and do not need me."

She entered into what seemed like a mystical communion with them from which he was obviously excluded. Despite the maids and the big house, she seemed to rediscover something in the process of motherhood that had been absent for too long. She lavished all her love on the boys and appeared not to notice the unfocused look of acquired beatitude she sometimes perceived in her husband's face. She must have known this meant that he had been searching, yet again, for spiritual ecstasy through the channel of the physical—and not, she could swear, with her. As a replacement for his love and her talent (neither of which she seemed to need any longer) she developed a symphonic passion for food. Occasionally, out of duty, he lifted her night-dress, and she, wearily, played with him just enough for them to be able to simulate the love they had once felt. That was how Francisco was conceived, long after the twins might have enjoyed his playful company.

Then, as if in some warped echo of that composer's life, her twins had been taken away from her, and her life emptied messily around her, making her doubt all her old beliefs, convulsing her with guilt, and leaving Francisco, the third child, with the certain knowledge of withheld love. When Jacinto, who also loved his firstborn sons, returned from a concert tour and his pale wife, substantial but wraith-like, told him where they had gone he was inchoate with grief and did his best to get them back.

The sect they had joined, both at exactly the same time on the same day was a mysterious cult called the Sons of Perpetual Light. This cult persuaded all its members that previous ties of flesh and love were dispensable, and that divorce from such outdated kinship models was obligatory. They kept their followers behind high walls and knew how to avoid the kidnapping agents sent by distraught relatives to retrieve their lost members.

It was no good asking the authorities, either. The twins were of legal age. The leader of the sect was fabulously wealthy and had contacts with the ruling elites. There was nothing even a noted virtuoso like Professor Jacinto Perez could do. Once they thought they saw the boys on the streets of the capital, shaven-headed and wearing shifts like nightdresses as they danced along in a group of fifteen young men. But they could not be sure, and before they could stop the car to run over to them, they had vanished round a corner. When, ten minutes later, Jacinto and his out-of-breath wife ran to where the pilgrims had last been seen there was no sign of them. They were lost.

That was several years ago. Since then, Jacinto and Marisa,

musical stars and one-time stellar lovers, had settled into a destructively bleak acerbity. His life was fuelled by glimpses of unreliable ectasy. Her existence was marked by a strange translucent otherness, almost like a clinical complaint. Francisco, spotty and hunched, had fallen mostly silent, He played electronic music as loud as possible, presumably because it was the most blatant assault he could make upon his parents' classical tradition. He probably masturbated all the time. At least, his father thought, he looked as if he did.

He looked over at him now. The boy was hardly eating and his gaze appeared to be resolutely fixed to the table top. Jacinto was conscious of Marisa's penetrating glance from one to the other of them. She knew that something had happened between the father and his unloved son. But even she was not about to break into the cloying silence of the dining room. It would have taken an act of supreme obdurateness to do that.

Without wishing to—because he desperately did not want to— he found himself suddenly replaying the scene in his office earlier in the day. He nearly choked on his food. He heard again his son's unmistakable wheeze behind him, and realised how, in shock, he had jumped back out of his student, leaking everywhere because he couldn't help it. Meanwhile, she, obeying some time-honoured script, pulled an arm across her breasts and thrust her other hand between her legs. She gasped and blushed scarlet.

By this time, Jacinto was already hopping dementedly into his boxer shorts, ignoring the mess. He heard voices in the corridor outside his room.

"Christ!" he exploded at his son, panic lending viciousness to his voice. "Shut the fucking door, Francisco. Don't just stand there!"

When he looked round, having got his trousers on and reaching for the shirt which he had discarded casually across the sofa arm, his son had not moved. He stood rooted to the spot, his mouth half open, a blank stare in his short-sighted eyes which were still full of the sight of his father's hairy backside, the folds of his ample back.

The professor had no idea what to do. He could not meet Angelita's eyes because he was confused. He did not know how to tell her, in front of his son, that he might be married, but also that he believed in love, and he worshipped her. The situation was too awful for that kind of thing. So he just ignored her while he tried to work out how to restore some semblance of normality to this grotesque scene.

He need not have bothered. A second later, Francisco turned on his heel and ran from the room, making strange guttural sounds and slamming the door behind him. Angelita had cried a little and he had kept silent because he was so appalled. He sensed her pulling on clothes behind him. When she said goodbye all he managed was "my son," as if that would explain everything; no other words came. Poor girl. Oh God, if he could just see her again and tell her what was in his heart. He'd do it the moment he saw her again. If he saw her again. He was no fool.

For now he sat becalmed and isolated in their cold dining room eyrie, terrified of the consequences of his behaviour, yet almost in tears with the memory of the girl's sublime perfection just before the door had opened. He knew it was an illusion. "Godammit, I'm middle-aged after all. But I want something to believe in. That girl could give me life," he said quietly, to no one but himself.

Somehow, they all struggled through their food. At least the adults did. The atmosphere became even more oppressive. Any moment now, the professor thought, Francisco is going to explode. God knows what he will say. "Excuse me my dear," he said as soon as it was possible. "I just have to go and check the score for tomor-row's concert." (He was conducting the city orchestra in the National Auditorium.) "I won't be long."

His wife did not say, "But you know this music by heart," or, "But you haven't had any cheese yet." She just let him go, watching him leave from her faraway eyes. Later, as he sat in his music room, the score open but unread upon his knees, the city spread-eagled with obscene abandon twenty-three storeys beneath him, he breathed a huge sigh of relief and wondered how long he could stay in this room, safe, untroubled by his own betrayal or, if he had only realised it, by his own grief.

Angelita

ANGELITA WATCHED her father finish his beer—his second, as usual —and then saw him wipe his mouth with the back of hand, as usual, before putting his beer mug down on the table and sitting back with a contented sigh. He had wiped his plate clean with the chunks of *bolillo* which they usually bought to accompany their meal.

"Not hungry?" he said, looking at her half-uneaten helping.

"Not really, Papa," she said. She still felt sick-hearted and confused from the events of the morning. Worse, she knew she had been unable to hide her sense of disorientation from her loving father. Yet now she knew that this was something she could not talk about, because he would not understand how she could have done it. No one could.

"Are you all right?" he asked again, his eyes searching for a chink through which he might catch a glimpse of her soul. It was some time since he had seen her this troubled.

"Yes, Papa, I am fine," she lied, adding with a semblance of that private look she used to ward off his unwelcome enquiries. "It's just, you see, not a particularly good day for me. Okay?" She even felt guilty when she saw him get the message that he was asking her about mysteries from which he was permanently excluded.

"I see," he harrumphed. "Well, anyway, that was a nice dinner. Thank you. I'm sorry you didn't enjoy it more yourself. I mean if you really are all right."

"Relax, Papa, I'm fine," she insisted. "Do you want more yourself?"

"Two helpings is enough for any man," he laughed, reaching out for his pack of cigarettes. "You don't want your old man to get all *gordo*, do you?"

"No, I don't want him to get fat. I also don't want him to get all wheezy and die from smoking too much either," she snapped back more harshly than she intended. Her nerves were on edge.

"Don't start! Not again. Truly, daughter, I've got to have some pleasures in life. Allow me one vice at least." He lit his cigarette and got up abruptly, moving away from the table to stand over by the window.

The atmosphere was wrong. They both knew it, yet neither of them knew how to do anything about it. Angelita was nearly at the end of her tether, sickened but half seduced by the piquancy of her stupidity. Federico was aware that he was being shut out. It annoyed him. He went over to the television and switched it on. He could not bear to sit down and relax so he stood there, pretending to watch a popular entertainer who mimicked a child's voice from his man's body. They both knew he despised him. He did not help his daughter take the dishes to the kitchen.

When she came back to the room, having dried up and put everything away, he had turned off the television and sat in his armchair reading a book of poetry he frequently turned to. It was full of passion, struggle, and the pain of sacrifice. He looked up over the half-moon glasses he had recently been forced to start wearing. He stared hard at his beautiful daughter, willing her to smile at him.

After a moment he asked, "Are you gonna practise? You've only got an hour or so." He meant before it would be anti-social for her scales and arpeggios to ring out over the diminishing roar of the night traffic. He might have looked askance at her dedication to music, but he had got used to the sound of her violin in the evening.

"Not tonight," she said, her voice flat to his unmusical ears. "I'm going to bed, Papi, if you don't mind." In her bedroom she could close the door and hide behind it. She would bury her head in the pillow and push her discomfort away.

"I don't mind, *mi princesa*. I don't mind anything you do. Well, not much of it anyway." If he knew—if he only knew. "Just so long as you're OK."

"Love you, Papa," she said, coming over to him and kissing him on his stubbly cheek.

"Sleep well," he mumbled, patting her side, then holding her arm for just a minute. "I only want your happiness. You know that."

"Yes, I do." Another wave of shame lashed its sand into her. "Good night," she whispered, and walked back along the corridor.

Her phone rang just as she reached her room. A moment of panic. He wouldn't dare. Not after that, would he? She looked down at the screen and was instantly overcome with relief.

"Angelita?"

"Yes," she replied, trying to inject colour into the monochrome of her voice.

"Hey, what's the matter? You OK? It's me," the caller announced confidently.

"Of course it's you, Julio. How are you?"

"You weren't at school," Julio protested. "We were going to meet. You remember? After my lesson? Which I didn't have by the way. The old goat cancelled at the last moment. Something about his not being well, the secretary said, but I'm sure I saw him leaving later. It's not that I mind missing out on his scary sarcasm, but I've been practising like a demon, and I had to get an early plane down for this as well. I read through one of Yolanda's pieces. Almost impossible to play—quarter tones, all that stuff. But it's kind of mystical, as usual. Sometimes that girl frightens me, I mean I know that she's..." He stopped, conscious of the silence echoing down the line. "Angelita," he was forced to say. "Are you there?"

"What? Yes. Sorry."

"Come on, Angelita. Where were you anyway?"

"I came back home," she said, as if that explained everything.

"Yes, I've got that. But why?

"Julio," she countered. "Are you staying with your uncle, or what?"

"With my Tio Ernesto, as always."

His uncle worked in the library of the national university and lived on the other side of the city.

"Do you want to come into town for a drink?" he asked.

"No," she breathed. "No, I can't. I'm going to bed."

"Bed? At this hour? You ill or something?"

"Or something. I, it's difficult... can we meet up tomorrow?"

"Sure, if you want. I've got classes off. Hey, you know when I've got classes, right? Same time as yours."

"Yes. But Julio, not at the school, OK? Can we meet at the café, at say 11:15?"

"Sure. If that's what you want."

"Please. I don't think I can go into school tomorrow."

"Why not? What's happened?"

"It's a long story. Well, no, actually, it's a short story. And a boring story. Doesn't matter. See you at 11:15?"

"Yeah, OK. Hey, Angelita?"

"What?"

"Are you coming to San Miguel for the celebrations?" Julio was a Migueleño. She had first met him there many years ago when she was on holiday at her grandfather's. She had been thrilled when her friend had decided, like her, to study music.

"Celebrations?" Her voice sounded hollow.

"*¡Dios mío!* Angelita. The Volcano birthday. Are you coming up for that?"

"I don't know," she offered. "I haven't really decided. I might." She remembered that she didn't want to disappoint him. "Look," she said, "I'm sorry. Really sorry. I'm just not feeling too good. I'll see you tomorrow, OK?"

"Yes, I suppose so." He rang off. One part of her brain knew exactly how he felt and was sorry for it. Right now, though, there was nothing she could do.

Victoria

"HELLO? VICKY?"

"Martin. Hello." She thought that she couldn't talk to her brother right now. She had to sort this situation out first. She wished it had been Alex.

"What do you think of it?"

"What do I think of what?"

"Oh, come on. My story, of course."

"Martin! I haven't had time to read it yet. You only left it here last night."

"Oh, yes. I suppose I did. I just hoped you'd had a chance to give it a bit of a look. That's all." He sounded crushed. She could almost see his reproachful expression accusing her down the line. But really, she'd put up with him until three in the morning. She'd been almost asleep when he rang, but she'd humoured him anyway, and let him come over.

Couldn't he leave her in peace just for once? She was off-balance, suddenly angry at him. No, that wasn't fair. It wasn't his fault that she was in this present predicament.

"Look Martin, I'm sorry all right. I will read it, I promise you, and I'll give you my honest opinion, OK?"

"When?"

"Martin!"

A voice from upstairs. "Mummy, I can't sleep." It was Daniel, the oldest. She could tell that he was standing at the top of the stairs. "I'll be up in a minute, Danny, go back to bed. I'm talking to Uncle Martin."

"Mummy!" She heard the feather of his footfall as he started down the first steps.

"Daniel!" she shouted imperiously, holding the phone away from her face. "Get back to bed this instant or I won't come at all." There was a silence. Then she heard his little feet pad reluctantly away, back to his room. He must have realised that she meant business. She only called him Daniel when she was cross or otherwise resolute.

"Vicky," she heard her brother complaining when she lifted the phone to her ear again. "Can I come round?"

Again? She couldn't face another late night. She wouldn't have anything to say which might help him. She feared the blank fog of his uncertainty. On bad days, his egotistical pain could drain the life out of her so that even when she managed to cheer him up she was left feeling abandoned herself.

It hadn't always been like this. When he had first come here, following her in order to be close to the only family he had left, she had laughed at the way he had fallen for the place just as she herself had done. Then, he had taught himself to tolerate Alex in his own way. He had been content to learn the language, give language classes himself, and later, to pick up translation work. All the time she had acted as his base, his anchor, his counsellor, and, on too many occasions, his bank. Alex, who came from a family of independent siblings, occasionally complained about his brother-in-law's frequent presence and continual demands, but he knew their history and recognised his wife's pain at being torn between the two people she loved. He backed away and learned, almost, to enjoy the younger man's company.

When Martin stopped coming round so often, Vicky was hurt at first by the way a girlfriend called Margarita seemed to have taken her place. But when she realised why she felt like this, she reproached herself for resenting precisely the situation she had hoped would come about.

It didn't help that she found Margarita difficult and feared that she had only latched on to her brother as a drowning woman reaches for a lifebelt. For example, it was difficult to watch Martin handling her so reasonably and gently when she had again had too much to drink. Yet in holding up someone so much more needy than himself, Martin seemed to have become more solid. His eyes lost their shifty look. He redirected his gaze from the emptiness of his own soul to the engulfing chaos of someone else's precariousness. For that Vicky was profoundly grateful. But then, once Margarita had gone—and like that—he came flying back into his sister's life even worse than before. He was lonely, resentful and now robed in coruscating guilt. If it hadn't been for the children whose needs made first claim upon her emotional energies, or Alex who reignited her hope for life's varied potential every time he gazed at her, Martin might have dragged her back to the time before, to the shotgun echoes in her head. There was only so much she could take.

"Look, Martin," she began again, thinking that she had to do this carefully, poor Martin, she couldn't have him thinking she'd given up on him. "Look, I've got a bit of a problem on my hands right now which I have to sort out. Can it wait?"

"Can't I help you?" her brother asked in return. She knew he could not. What, after all, would he say to the woman perched uncomfortably in the room she normally dusted? Martin would have no comfort to offer the battered wife who slumped on the cushions she was more accustomed to shake and pound back into shape.

There was nothing he could offer to this woman who had turned up an hour ago. She had wept slowly and persistently since Vicky had led her, unresisting, into the house. It had seemed wrong to take her into the kitchen where she spent so much of her time. There was no space to tend to her in the maid's room. It didn't seem right to take her to the playroom either. The clutter of children's toys seemed too frivolous for the healing of such obvious distress. So they had come to the elegant sitting room, a place where both of them felt the maid to be out of place.

As she tried to discover what had brought Maria to this state—though she supposed she knew—Vicky found herself, without thinking, sitting side-by-side with the snivelling woman. She put her arm around her soft shoulders and stroked her hair, offering up a constant supply of tissues whilst all the time murmuring gentle words of comfort and encouragement. Sometimes Maria would become calm. Once or twice, she was able to look round at her employer and then Vicky saw in the swimming eyes a look of desperation, but a hint of defiance, too, as if she resented being looked after in this way. Then the weeping would start again, and there was no more resistance to Señora Bicky's comforting arms.

Shortly before Martin rang, Vicky had realised that she would have to do something drastic if she was to get anywhere with her unexpected visitor. She thought of shouting at her, slapping her or shaking her—the kind of thing that happened in films and novels. But she didn't have the nerve. Instead she got up, leaving the slumped woman crouched into the sofa, and went to the cupboard where they kept their drinks. She poured a large measure of brandy, thinking, wryly, that it was a pity they did not have a national variety available given the price of imported brands. She took the glass to Maria, and forced her to take a large sip.

The effect was dramatic and immediate. Maria, who had never drunk alcohol before, sat up straight, her eyes almost exploding out of her skull, and started to gag as if she could not breathe. Suddenly alarmed, Vicky slapped her on the back, then regretted her action as precious liquid cascaded out of the glass and over the maid's hands.

Maria stopped coughing. Before she had time to think about it, Vicky made her drink again. She offered more tissues and watched Maria wipe her flooded eyes. She cleared her throat. She turned to her employer, and in a voice low and urgent, she said, "Señora, do you think God will forgive me?"

"For what?" Vicky replied, hardly daring to ask, now that an explanation seemed to be about to present itself.

"What would our blessed Mary, the sainted mother of Jesus Christ say to a woman like me? How could I ever bring myself to look her in the face?"

"Maria," she said quietly now, trying not to be too harsh. "Maria, why wouldn't you be able to look the sainted Mary in the face?"

"When you take your vow, forever, before God, to honour a husband, to serve him, in sickness and in health, can it ever be right to leave him?"

"That depends, I think, on what your reasons are and on what he might have done to you."

"If he treats you worse than a mule, if he behaves as if you were a scavenging dog? If he humiliates you day after day. If you start, God help me, to wonder how he who has made us allows this?"

"Why then…" Vicky started carefully. But, at that moment, the telephone rang. Now here she was, trying to stop her brother from joining her employee on the sofa.

"Martin look, please just this once, please. It's Maria." She was almost whispering, though she knew the maid would not understand her and that, anyway, she wasn't listening.

"Well, if your maid's more important than your own brother!"

Vicky was suddenly absolutely furious. She felt battered and abused by anyone who felt like it. Suddenly strident, she shouted, "Enough!" into the phone. "Enough, Martin. That's it. I've had it." She was conscious of Maria moving on the sofa, turning round to look at her, and this helped to dampen the choler which had suddenly invaded her.

"Christ!" she heard her brother protest like a hurt schoolboy. "I just wanted someone to talk to, that's all."

"Martin look, I'm sorry, OK. It's been a long day. I didn't get any sleep last night and now I've got a really important problem on my hands and… oh no, Danny's awake, I'd forgotten. Please, please. We'll talk tomorrow, OK. You'll be all right until tomorrow?"

"I saw a girl on the metro this afternoon," he said as if she had not spoken, "and for a moment I thought, I even felt…."

"What? What did you feel?"

"I've decided to go back there," he announced. "Back where?" What on earth was he talking about? "To San Miguel. I'm going back to San Miguel."

She would have spoken, but at that moment Maria, who had carelessly tipped the rest of the brandy down her throat, started to choke again, so that Martin was left unsatisfied as his sister hung up the phone in order to avert another catastrophe.

Jacinto

HE REMEMBERED a day during a holiday they had taken together some years ago. Marisa, already comfortable-looking, but not yet monumental, had disliked the heat and glitter of the resort, Siete Vientos, that he had chosen on the spur of the moment. She yearned for something more restrained, somewhere with more cultural history, something altogether quieter than the rabid timpani of the Pacific sun. She was not attracted by the shouted excess of a resort in its prime.

It was before the famous hurricane which almost wiped the place out. Jacinto, however, mindful of his young twins' enthusiasms and pumped up by the constant travelling of the last few years, craved the whistles at Esquivel's restaurant and the glittering refraction of ice cubes in exotic cocktails. He longed to laugh at the boys' screams of pleasure as they bounced over the waves on the newly introduced inflatable bananas that were yanked chaotically behind surging launches. He loved their shrieks of excitement as they ran down into the sea. When, through their eyes, he watched the perfect-bodied divers launch themselves into space for their muscular swallow dives, their admiration of physical triumph made him remember his own childhood.

Jacinto had needed something to counter the refined passion of his professional travels. He wanted to violate the focused control that was demanded of him when he launched into another concerto in some foreign capital, playing to acclimatised audiences who, as likely as not, knew every note and demanded that he play them all in the ways they were accustomed to. The fathering of children seemed a perfect foil; two rumbustious boys, still, at that time, disorganised and curious, cymbal discords to his strict harmony (except when, with their mother, their eyes suddenly went silent into secrets he was startlingly denied). What better, then, than a holiday of light and noise, of wonderful chaos as an antidote to sublime precision?

One night from that holiday stuck in his mind. The hotel had offered a traditional fiesta, all bubbling *casuelas* of earthy sauces and dancers with their flowing finery. The men wore silver-studded pants. Red cravats splattered their white shirts. The women were immaculately erotic in their billowing butterfly skirts, their black hair tight curled and bedecked with ribbons. The boys cheered and clapped, happy to be allowed to stay up with them in the tropical night. Marisa, seeing their happiness, and for once sharing them generously with her husband, laughed and giggled, her eyes shining in the candlelight. For a moment it felt as it should, he thought, the four of them united in excitement. Cooking smells wafted over them in the evening air. The sea winked its phosphorescence at them and a bright moon hung over the bay.

The hotel guests were seated in a large semi-circle by the pool, beyond which a stage had been erected for their entertainment. There was a band of musicians made up of guitarists, trumpeters, and violinists. There were harmony choruses to punctuate the ecstatic tenor of the soloist. There was the violins' smooth carpet to moderate the trumpets' boisterous percussion. The dancers swirled and pirouetted in the soft air.

The dancers stopped after a bit and then the band put down their instruments and went for a break. The main course was served by waiters costumed in different styles from around the republic. They ate and talked happily. They were sitting at a table with a foreign family from far to the north. Marisa had to translate for the boys, who had not yet started to study that language. Jacinto watched them as they struggled between elation and exhaustion, and caught his wife's eye, knowing that she was thinking exactly the same.

The band returned, but instead of starting to play, they stood while the lead singer came up to the microphone. *"Señoras y señores,"* he said, "I have been told that we have among us this evening…"

Jacinto knew what was coming and looked over to Marisa, raising an ironic eyebrow.

"The great violin virtuoso, the maestro Don Jacinto Perez." The singer stopped, looking around the audience, not having been told where he was sitting. "Maestro Perez *¡por favor!"* he shouted enthusiastically. Even then, Jacinto might have ignored him, but his twin sons had identical smiles of excitement on their faces and Marisa was laughing at him. He stood up and bowed towards the stage. The foreigners at his table gasped. One of the musicians called to a technician and a spotlight spun towards him. Now there was nothing for it and he bowed and waved, this way and that, to the applauding guests, musicians and waiters. He didn't know whether to feel amused or irritated.

The spotlight moved away and he made to sit down, but the singer had not finished. "Maestro," he invited, "it will be for us a great honour to have you play a tune with our humble band. Ladies and gentlemen, is this not a good idea?"

They all yelled *"Sí,* yes, yes!" The boys were yelling, too. Marisa chuckled, "Tthere's no getting out of this now." He looked at the three of them, smiled, and surrounded by applause, walked around the pool until welcoming arms helped him up onto the stage. One of the violinists handed him an instrument, a pedestrian thing, Jacinto knew, with a bow so much less perfect than his own.

"Maestro," he pleaded, obsequiously, "it would be an honour for me if you would play my humble instrument." He took it, and when the band launched into 'La Rebelde', an old revolutionary song about a passionate woman, he played with a wild sentimentality quite unlike his normal controlled ecstasy. He alternated solos with the singer, swaying for all the world like a pop star.

When the song ended, and he finished on a triumphant up-bow, horsehair flying silver in the lights, the diners stood and cheered. Because he was so happy, he in turn called Marisa to the rickety stage. She sang the 'Song of the Swallows' in a voice so penetrating and so sweet that he could hardly play himself. When she duetted with his violin or made perfect harmony with the over-awed musicians, the silent mystery that she so often disappeared into sloughed off her like unwanted underwear. The night was full of their loving melody.

Afterwards, when they had kissed their sons goodnight, the boys hugged them with love and pride, falling asleep almost immediately, their peaceful faces suffused with belonging. Then, Marisa took her husband to the adjoining room and once she had struck off their encumbering clothes, pulled him into her and ground him into an apotheosis of suppressed ecstasy while the boys, deep in the sleep, dreamed of love and content.

Dear God, thought Jacinto Perez as he sat in his study many years later. It was after an uncomfortable dinner with his silently accusing other son. *How was that possible, then?* He wondered how he had got himself into his present situation, and how he had made such a mess of things. How could he have stopped those lovely boys from leaving them like that? How could he ever make Marisa happy again? He closed his eyes so that the room should not see him. He sighed uncontrollably, wracked with self-pity. He felt the prosecution's stare. He saw himself as a pariah, banned from the society of the honourable and the good. For how, he told himself in a practised ritual of self-abnegation that was a familiar counterpoint to his libidinous sensuality, can I ever show my face again, least of all to myself when the mirror is held up?

The phone in his pocket started to ring, startling him so that he knocked the score he had been pretending to study off his knees onto the floor. "Yes," he barked when he had retrieved his mobile, unsettled because he had not completed his personal cycle of reproach and redemption. "Yes?"

"Maestro," a voice answered, clearly apprehensive after his aggressive growl. "Jacinto, it's me, Marisol Cardova. Are you all right?"

"Of course I'm all right," he nearly shouted back. "Why shouldn't I be?"

"Are you going to ask me how I am?"

He softened then because her voice was provoking a fond memory. "I am sorry," he said more softly. "You caught me at a bad moment, that's all. How are you?" He owed her that at least, remembering the heavy scent that had lain on her soft skin.

"I am fine. I am to be married soon."

Something was expected of him so he said, "Congratulations. That's marvellous. Lucky man. Who is he? Do I know him?"

"You might know him," she suggested, "if you do the favour I am going to ask of you."

"Favour? What favour?" He panicked for a moment, wondering what manner of trial she might be about to put him through. "Where are you calling from anyway?" he asked, to buy himself more time.

"From San Miguel, of course. Where else?"

"Of course. Well? Please go on."

"Have you heard about the volcano?" she asked, her tone changing so that she sounded both efficient and considerate.

"Well yes Marisol my dear, of course I have. I have been there before, you know. That is, I mean...." He had no wish to embarrass her or himself.

"No, you silly man," she chided him, removing the sting, "I mean have you heard about our volcano festival? The Volcano Birthday, they are calling it. You know, to celebrate its fiftieth year."

"I heard something about it. It's in about two or three weeks, isn't it?"

"That's right. Two and a half weeks from now."

"So what is the favour?" though by now he had a pretty good idea.

"We had... I don't know how to put this without it coming out all wrong, and I wouldn't have rung you if it hadn't been for our previous, mmm, contact..."

"All right, all right. What is your problem?"

"We had a concert lined up for the first night. An orchestra from across the ocean..." She named a band that made him gasp with admiration, a band he'd played with only twice before. "But they've suddenly cancelled. The arrangements weren't quite right. Money, or something like that. Frankly, that leaves us in a terrible mess."

"And you want me to jump in and bail you out?"

"Something like that."

"But why are you calling? What's your part in all of this?"

"I'm on the organising committee of the festival. It's going to be great fun you know—well it will be if we can keep the religious nuts and the weirdos away. You'd love it. We'd look after you. We can't pay you much, of course. San Miguel's not that rich. But as a favour?" Her voice tailed off.

"Let me get this straight," Jacinto said, blushing as his wife popped her head round the door and informed him that she was going to bed as coolly as only she knew how. "You want me to come to San Miguel as a second best, to play for a bunch of freaks. Is that it?"

"Oh dear," she said, and something in her voice suddenly vouchsafed him a fleeting memory of her innocent nudity. "I shouldn't have said that about the weirdos. It's only one lot we're worried about, really, the 'Sons of Perpetual Light' they call them-selves. But they're…"

"Who?" he interrupted. "Who did you say?"

"The Sons of Perpetual Light," she repeated, puzzled, "They're some kind of religious sect or cult or something. Why?"

"They're going to be at this festival of yours?"

"Well, yes. I think so. That's the rumour. They're very secretive. But someone in the town hall says that apparently there's something special about the volcano. It's got some special mystical significance for them. Don't worry, though, I'm sure they won't be any bother, honestly, and the security at the festival…"

"Marisol," he interrupted for the second time, "it's all right. No need to go on. I may just be able to help you after all."

Part Two

Preparations

Alexei

ALEXEI WOKE up with thumping pain hammering all over his head. Licking his impossibly dry lips he wondered where on earth he was and why he was lying half on and half off a bed with one boot on and one boot off. His shorts appeared to be partially unbuttoned and there was a damp patch beside him. A container must have leaked its contents all over the sheets.

Sun poured into the room, but when he tried to raise his head and look out of the window, the spears of pain which skewered his eyeballs made him burrow back into the pillow which lay crumpled and disorganised beneath his ear. With great bravery he forced himself to make a minute gap between two lids of one throbbing eye and brought his watch up to his face. After a period of contemplation he worked out that it was half-past five, and since the sun was apparently hot and potent, he deduced that it was afternoon.

He realised that he needed to urinate—desperately. With the urgency of this need heavy upon his bodily senses, he ignored the chemical roars of protest from his suffering cerebellum, rolled off the bed, and started to make his way to where he somehow knew the bathroom was, even though it seemed to him that he might never have been in this room before. Then again, he might have.

His shorts slipped down his legs at this point and nearly tripped him up. He half fell to his knees. He was obliged to shake his head to try to clear his brain. Realising that he needed to hurry to prevent some kind of accident, he stumbled upright and crawl-walked to the lavatory like a naughty schoolboy. Finally he stood there, swaying dramatically against the wall, while he exercised the residue of his sense of balance—and a lot of concentration—to keep his aim appropriately true.

When this ordeal was over, and feeling now a bit better, he managed to re-fasten his shorts successfully, leave the bathroom and walk back into the bedroom. There was a plastic bottle by the bedside. He was sure it contained nothing but water, and wrenching the top off he tipped the contents down his throat, his Adam's apple oscillating wildly as he did his best to counter the crippling dehydration which was afflicting him.

Now he was able to look around the hotel room. This had been his home for the last three weeks, but it had rarely looked as in disarray as it did now. His leather shoulder bag was discarded by the door; the chair which normally stood at the table was on its side; and the clothes which had before neatly decorated it were now scattered on the floor. The door to the terrace was open in the afternoon heat, while the bedclothes were all bunched and disorganised.

Gingerly, he picked up a beer bottle from the rumpled covers and took it over to the table. Then with a supreme effort, he bent down and righted the chair, collecting his clothes from the frayed carpet before dropping them in a heap on the seat.

As his personality reasserted itself, he was able to remember where he was. He went out onto the terrace to escape the evidence of abandon in the room behind him. He pulled a cheap pair of dark glasses from his shirt pocket and thrust them in front of his battered eyes. Now he could afford to let his gaze wander over the spectacular view before him, a view that he thought he would never tire of.

In front of him, down the slope, was the old church, attached to the abandoned convent where once nuns had prayed, raw-kneed, for the salvation of their souls, yearning for the fire of God's love as they tended their garden and chanted their plainsong orisons. Now bats flew in and out of its hallowed spaces and the plaster mildewed just a bit more every rainy season. There weren't any nuns any longer because sometime around a hundred and fifty years ago, the country's cardinal, Don Ocatavio Villacampo y Villacampo, had closed the place down.

This happened once he had been apprised of the favours which the women of the order had felt obliged to offer to visiting clergy and various local notables, partaking of an earthly rather than a spiritual paradise in a time of drought and pestilence. More recently, once the convent had been permitted to reopen by one of Villacampo y Villacampo's successors, it had fallen victim to a post-revolutionary fervour when priests were persecuted, nuns were abused, and the wearing of any Christian uniform outside of cathedrals and churches was forbidden, an order not yet rescinded despite protests both national and international. This was in a country whose people manifested a deep religiosity. Such contradictions were eternally fascinating to a visitor like Alexei.

The convent was still abandoned. A succession of uses for it had been proposed by the council, but they had all foundered because the church leaders were unable to decide either on secular projects, such as an art gallery, or on a new religious use. The church, on the other hand, all distressed stone on the outside, masking the gold-leaf excess of its interior, was still very much in use. Its twin towers dominated the market square at this end of Buena Vista which clung to the edges of San Miguel, its larger neighbour. It still resisted becoming just another suburb. They stood out against the dramatic hills and mountains which ran along two sides of the valley in which San Miguel had been founded. Beyond them San Miguel itself was struggling to become a real city, not just a big town. In the distance there were occasional high buildings whose glass hides glinted in the afternoon sun. From where Alexei stood he could hear the hum of traffic below him. An ambulance or police car hee-hawed its way from his left to his right.

But then the voice started again (he had been unaware of it before), amplified, and seemingly directed straight at him, as it bounced off all the surfaces around. He realised what day it was—market day. That meant the presence of Fulgencio Revueltos, the charlatan, a person Alexei had come to hate in only three weeks.

Today, for the third time since Alexei had arrived, Revueltos had hung up a loud-hailer from the top of a pole outside the church, and from early morning Alexei suspected (though he had been almost permanently unconscious for most of that time) the man had shouted his imprecations, sometimes taped to save his voice, forcing his appallingly repetitive nostrums on everyone for miles around.

Alexei already knew the script from Mr Revueltos' previous visits. "Señora," went the braying voice, "come to visit me here so that I can show you here, with just two or three drops, the cure that awaits you and señor, step up too so that I can tell you in all confidence, of the magic of my *curamientos*, and the propaganda I am offering you señora, the propaganda I am offering you señor is so that you, too, may be aware of the efficacy of our treatments."

Hell, Alexei thought, *I'd like to murder that man.* He just sits there behind his stall offering remedies that even he must know are useless. What must it do to a man's soul to know that he is lying, that his lies are reverberating around the hills and valleys of this astonishing country. Or perhaps he has told the story so many times he has even come to fool himself into a semblance of belief. Like people who write horoscopes, all that astrological mumbo-jumbo. What about all those cults with crazy leaders? The leaders can't really swallow the blasphemies they force feed to their followers, can they?

Last week Alexei had spoken to an old woman, white-haired and prune-wrinkled like a wise ornament, who had a silver stall. When he asked her if señor Revueltos' cures were any good, she rolled her eyes dramatically. "Well, señor," she said laconically, "it is difficult to know. Some are, perhaps. Some are not." He wanted to ask her, to press her. Which were the ones that worked? The treatments for haemorrhoids or flatulence? The liquids for impotence or kidney malfunction? Or perhaps it was the powder to help students to concentrate at school, eat better, or stop urinating when they shouldn't, which the old quack should be proudest of.

Fulgencio Revueltos had now got to the part, repeated over and over again during the course of one day, that made Alexei angriest. "And now señora, now señor," the megaphone boomed, "I have the honour to be presenting to you this very day señora, this very day señor, the one and only Cat's Claw powder. If you have cancer, señora, if you have irregularity of the liver, señor, if you hair is thinning, if you have the pain of the knees or your hips do not work señora, or if you have trouble with your private parts, Cat's Claw powder taken daily señora, with regularity señor, will lighten your load and ease your predicament. I tell you no lie, señora, if I say that I am known throughout the republic for this great medical advance. I can say with total confidence, señor, that my Cat's Claw powder has been on television..."

On and on went the cheating voice, so loud it seemed to burrow into the vulcanologist's hungover brain, violating his senses with its denial of everything the scientist in him knew to be rational. He felt his heart fill with rage and this time, he was sure, he would do what he had dreamed of last week: he would march down there into the market with his knife and sever the remedy-seller's speaker cable in at least six separate pieces shouting all the time, "And my ears that have been assaulted all day by your rubbish, with your lies? What cure do you have for that you cheating bastard?"

Suddenly, to add to the incessant gabbling from the megaphone, a bell started to clang from the church, its percussive echo like some hideous counterpoint to the potion seller's melody. Alexei could just make out a young man in the tower operating the mechanism, *boing-boing-boing.* He wondered about his ears, almost certainly traumatised with all that noise reverberating, it seemed, only a few inches away from his head.

He wanted to consider his morning's drinking and work out how on earth he had managed to get so inebriated. But this dual assault upon his hearing allowed him no time for reflection, only confusion and displacement. As if directed against himself, specifically, a loudspeaker crackled into life, situated somewhere near the bell-ringer, Alexei supposed.

"*Alleluia, Alleluia,*" wailed the voice of a priest. "The Lord is with you. Come to him, all of you who are heavy-laden and need his love."

That's it, Alexei mused, shaking his head in disbelief in the afternoon. That's the whole gloomy story. All this noise, all those broadcast voices shattering my calm, offering instant remedies for our failings and perturbations. It's too much. If the people down there don't surrender to one of them, they'll roll over into submission in front of the other. Or, they'll go for both just to be on the safe side. I prefer the old gods of this place if I have to show a preference for any gods at all. I'll put my faith in Tlacoltepeca, devourer, the rupturing earth, or Qualtixtlaqueña, the corn-giver, or Xenal the bringer of rain or Tsingxatl, the scorching sun. At least they stand for something solid, something observable rather than hangdog promises and protestations of altruistic love. If we have to create spirits at least let them be ones like these.

His thinking, he was sure, was not that different from people like Fukako and Tomoko—yes, now he remembered. They were both leaving this afternoon, going back to their own country because a university term was starting.

He'd heard that people from over there were not heavy drinkers, but by the gods of this valley, they'd drunk him into a stupor with their hot rice wine—taken after the large beers they had all drunk in preparation. And then, seated cross-legged to show politeness to the departing scientists, everyone poured each other's drinks as custom, Tomoko said, dictated, so that no-one beside you ever has an empty glass. Thus they had all got significantly drunk, the phenomenon observable as they swayed more, flailing their arms, while their voices got louder and louder. Alexei needed three or four tries to stand up when it was time to leave. Then he hugged Tomoko over and over again in alcoholic sentimentality.

"But I have to go, Alex," he was told when he urged them not to, the other's words falling like water on dry earth. "I want to stay and see this thing through—if we're right, that is, and it's going to blow. But science is money, dear friend, money is science. I have to go back. Even though I do not wish it." He lurched backward. Alexei moved with him. The two of them almost fell, but Tomoko was agile enough to push the bearded man away from him. "Remember, dear friend," he said, "not to be involved in the trouble, not to stick your neck out, however passionate you are. Volcanoes, not justice, are your work. Leave that to others who are skilled in the knowledge of right and wrong. For they will send you away if you are not careful and then you will have to leave as we now have to do." Then he burst into tears, and the last Alexei saw of him, through his deteriorating vision, was as he crawled away, shy-shouldered, arms wrapped round his companion for mutual support.

How he got back to his room, Alexei mused, trying to ignore the noise all around him, he had no idea, nor how he opened the door or fell on the bed. "God!" he shouted out loud, surprising himself considerably. "Why don't you shut up, you noisy sons of bitches!" Seconds later, to his astonishment, that is exactly what they did.

At first, it was just the fact that some dogs to his right who had been screaming at each other suddenly went quiet. The confused cockerels, who had a peculiar habit of crowing at about this time, failed to put in an appearance. Then, he felt something, not more than a little jolt beneath his feet. It could almost be put down to his own instability. But then it happened again.

The boy stopped ringing his bell, and the priest dried up, not being able to think of encouraging words quickly enough. Then, as the air filled with a distant rumbling, and Alexei, hanging on to the railing of his terrace, saw dust rise from the square, the loud hailer which Fulgencio Revueltos had used to publicise his wares, fell from its restraining nail to bounce onto the ground. Even the distant hum of traffic from San Miguel, over there, seemed to have been stilled. For once, as the trembling earth subsided, there was, for a moment, perfect silence. "Now," Alexei said, speaking in his mind as he always did at moments like this to his wife in the city (as if she could hear him). "Now it begins," and as he looked across the valley to where a wisp of smoke leaked up into the air, the *colonia* of Buena Vista came back to life with shouts of incredulity and salvation.

Genoveva

AT THE END of the night shift, weary from a lack of sleep, and her feet aching from the many miles she had walked up and down long wards and corridors, Genoveva Delgadillo Aceves, Julio's younger sister, entered the nurses' changing room. In front of her locker, she kicked off her shoes with a great sigh of pleasure. Lifting the keychain that disappeared into the utilitarian square pocket above her left thigh, she selected a key and unlocked the padlock that kept her possessions and civilian clothes safe behind the narrow metal door. She unbuttoned her dark blue uniform and picked a hanger from the mini-rail that hung in front of her. Pulling the recognisable symbol of her profession away from her tired body, she stretched it on the hanger and placed it inside.

For a moment, she stood there in her underwear, uncertain about what to do next. There were no other nurses around. Reaching forward, she peered at the watch still hanging from her uniform, and calculating that she had time to spare, she reached for her towel, repossessed her key ring, clamped the padlock shut, and hurried to the shower cubicles at the end of the room.

As usual, it took some time to get the temperature right. She had to stand on her tiptoes, stretching forward to turn on the taps. By gradually adding degrees of heat, the water reached a temperature to suit her needs. Casting aside her remaining clothes, she stepped into the warm stream of water and felt the individual jets from the battered old metal rose above her scatter their soothing fingers over her exhausted body.

Whenever she showered like this at the end of a long shift, she felt exhilarated, newly born almost. It was as if the mere fact of caressing droplets could revive stretched skin and clogged eyes, as if her cares and worries could be sluiced away as easily as she pointed her nose and closed eyelids at the water source and felt the liquid fly luxuriously to her face.

Genoveva stood there for what seemed like hours hardly moving, except by a shrug or new incline of a shoulder blade when she shifted almost imperceptibly and felt the water explore new channels and tributaries over her relaxing frame. When, from time to time, it seemed as if she were about to start thinking about her double life, triple even, caught between her job, her family, and the cause, she tipped her head even further back and pulled her fingers through her long hair, heavy and wet as it hung its weight down her back.

In the end, however, she realised that it was time to get on with her day. Suddenly decisive, she reached for the shower taps and turned them fiercely clockwise, but unevenly so that at the last moment she was lanced by a trickle of pure cold water. Then, for a second, the air around her was gloriously sharp and enervating, until, when it became noticeably frosty, she reached for her towel and dried herself vigorously, reddening the skin across her shoulders and around her waist in her enthusiasm. She wrapped the towel around herself and made her way back to her locker.

Two nurses had come into the room, and greeted her laconi-cally, their jealousy of her glowing relaxation quite apparent as they prepared to start their own long shifts. One of them was an ascetic short-haired woman whose caustic wit masked the obvious sympathy that only surfaced in her dealings with the patients. She watched Genoveva with disconcerting approval as she pulled jeans over her damp skin before tucking her denim shirt fiercely into her waistband. Still conscious of the others' scrutiny, she reached into her locker and fetched a brush which she dragged through her wet hair, revelling in the tugs at her scalp as drops of water cascaded to the floor, dampening her shirt as they went. Then Dolores, who had also been observing her, came up to her and frightened her more than she might have thought possible.

"Don't worry," she said, her hand brushing Genoveva's cheek, just like a caress. "Your secret is safe with me. Anyway, most of us here—even if not all—sympathise with what you people are trying to do." She winked and walked away, leaving Julio's sister standing there, her face stinging as if from an acid spill, and her mind racing with suspicious possibilities.

She hurriedly pulled on her trainers and reached into the locker for her bag before clanging the metal door shut and clamping the padlock once more. These were actions she had done many hundreds of times before, believing herself safe. But now? What was the point of the woollen head cover with its four little holes that slunk at the bottom of her bag? Why hide her identity, as they all did, if people knew who she was? Was this unmasking by the insistent Dolores a threat, and if so, to whom?

Genoveva had wanted to be a nurse for as long as she could remember. When, as a child, she had gone to visit her grandmother in hospital, she had been overwhelmed by the authority of the women who fussed around the old woman, comforting and organising her with no apparent fear for the fierce tyrant the young girl knew her father's mother to be. Later, when Julio had his accident and was thought to be in danger of disappearing completely before a surgeon's skill brought him back from almost certain death, Genoveva was entranced by what she now understood to have been the everyday professionalism of the care which nurses gave out to her unconscious brother and his terrified relatives. The image of that care never left her. When television shows featured nurses in their storylines she watched them avidly. By the time she left school she was adamant that this was what she wanted to be.

Her father was not happy with his daughter's decision. He had worked his way up from small farmer to his eminence as the head of a major producer of Blanquita, the national alcoholic drink. As his success had become more assured so he had started to harbour ambitions for his two children. "I came from humble beginnings," he would lecture them. "I got to where we are today, as a family, through a combination of good luck and perseverance." The siblings would stare up at the older man, his eyes heavy-lidded and keen, his plump hands coarse and ageing, and his masculine shoulders set hard above a powerful chest and trunk. When he started to talk like this, they knew that gravitas was expected of them, even though their mother, fine-boned and ethereal, where her husband was heavy-bodied and robust, would stand behind him, one eyebrow raised in ironic counterpoint.

"There is no point in us—in me—earning this money," he would intone, his eyes admonishing them one by one, "if the two of you end up having to work as hard as I have had to. I want you to have what I never had: the advantage of education. That is why your mother and I have made so many sacrifices to send you to the best schools. That is why you both will make of me a proud father—make us proud parents," he would add hastily, remembering whose authority he required to shore up his sermons.

Once he said, "In other languages, they call the alcohol we make a spirit, and it is a good word, I now understand. For the Blanquita spirit is flighty like a little bird, capricious like a woman's heart, changeable like the wind that blazes through the plains from the north and then rounds to flutter up the mountainsides. One day it comes out good. Another day the soul of this fire does not play by the rules which we wish to impose upon it. Like life. Like my life, which is uncertain and can be changed by the merest spirit of chance. It is this I do not wish to see in you—the suffering of life's chances. I wish to see for you good employment, secure employment, rich with the power of learning."

It took all their mother's kindness and blandishments, therefore, to soothe her husband's disappointment when Julio decided to study music. When Genoveva rejected administration and left her studies to pursue nursing he was again dumbfounded.

"She wants to be a nurse?" he thundered in surprise to his wife when Genoveva told them one Sunday lunch.

"Why yes, *mi amor*," her mother said, her soft brown eyes dancing in front of her husband's face. "What better calling can there be for us to be proud of? A child of ours who wishes to serve others?" She laid a hand on Ignacio's arm, talking him down, soothing him with her presence until the subject that had caused such controversy was almost forgotten.

My mother is like that, Genoveva thought remembering back to that day. Her mother was a tall woman, angular and slim. In repose her face sometimes had a planed sharpness, broken only by the laughter lines at the side of her eyes. But when she smiled and the lines became folds of happiness or merriment she was beautiful in her daughter's eyes, and in Don Ignacio's eyes, too, judging by the way he still looked at her after so many years, and by the way she managed to defuse his occasional panicked rages.

This time, though, it was different. Her father might have got used to his son the violinist—though his disappointment was moderated by his pride at the boy's obvious talent—and he might now accept his daughter the nurse, hoping that marriage might one day give her the kind of security that looking after sick people, in his eyes, did not.

But he would never, she was sure, understand her membership in the Ejercito de Arturo Sanchez—the EAS, as the 'army' was called. Nor would her mother be prepared to tolerate her activities as part of a group that to many symbolised a threat to their way of life, to their hard-won status. Yet that was not how Genoveva saw the campaign that she and her comrades were involved in. Their only motive was justice, not revenge. They wanted justice for the campesinos who worked the fields in the Valley of San Miguel, the long verdant plain stretching between the mountains and the far distant sea, where six powerful landowners kept a workforce enslaved and humbled, uneducated and permanently poor. Those landowners had side-stepped very forward-looking social law, every statement of rights and obligations, through their economic power, through the money they paid to the ruling party, and through the private armies they employed to police, at their own whim, their vast pastures and plantations. Rumours had recently begun to circulate, too, that in place of *maiz* and *maguey*, land was now set aside for other less legal crops, and that these landowners were rapidly amassing a different kind of power, a nastier kind of wealth.

While the town of San Miguel educated its children, and, with modest bribery here and there (most employers treated their workers with the semblance of fairness), not that many miles away —but a whole moral continent apart—gangster families like feudal lords operated with impunity, unfettered by the slow growth of social awareness elsewhere in the country.

"It is as if our revolution never happened," the man known only as Numero 22 said. It was the first time Genoveva had become aware of the EAS, when she happened upon one of their demonstrations by chance. "It is as if our grandfathers fought and died in vain," the speaker intoned, his bright eyes flashing behind the white wool of his balaclava. "Yet this cannot be. The people of this great country, the Indians who cultivated it, the invaders who took it from them and learned to cherish it in their turn, all of us, our bloods mingled together now, we all care about education and culture, food and light, warmth and shelter. We believe that they are our birthright, the birthright of all free men and women. And this is true for the humblest peon and the most exalted statesman. It is true for the shopworker and the soldier in his barracks; for the nurse at my hospital bedside and for the tourist waiter; for the driver of trucks and the pharmacologist behind his counter or the bank worker behind her counter. And listen, comrades, it is a truth that everybody in this wonderful land has learned at their mother's knee. We all know what our rights are, and how the lives of all of us should be. This is known by the worker in the fields and even our own president; it is known by the pancake-maker and even—though they pretend to ignore it—by the casiques, those abusers of power between the valley of San Miguel and the sea." The man's voice rang out over the crowd gathered uneasily in the main square, watched by a gang of armed police who looked uncertain about how to proceed.

"*Compañeros*," Number 22 yelled, "we are a proud nation, a modern nation, with history and culture, yet we are plagued by an illness, the spreading virus of corruption. With that evil of corruption comes the disease of cruelty and the abuse of power. It is this which we, the people, have to stamp out. Not by might of arms, or by the exercise of force, but by the power of our national conscience, by the hunger for justice for all our citizens that burns in the breast of every man and woman. For this cause we will make such a noise, we will make such music that those *ladrones*, those men in their overweening power, and the corrupt politicians who let them flourish, will say to all of us, *compañeros*, one nation in the cause of justice, we are sorry, we did not understand. We have wronged our people. We have wronged our mother country. Let us join you in your cause. Then we will open our arms and hold them to us, a people healed, a cause vindicated, a nation that can look itself in the face and say, yes, we are proud!"

"Who are you?" shouted a man from the edge of the crowd, a refrain taken up by others, suspiciously well-drilled, who stood around him.

"Who am I?" the speaker replied, his arms outstretched, crucifixion-high."Why, I am you." He pointed to the man who had first spoken."And you," he pointed to another. "And you, and you, and you," taking in the whole crowd before him. "I have lived a comfortable life, but I have ideals, too. That is why I have to do this. Like all my *compañeros* here." He gestured at the people around him on the rough platform, and at the crowd of his supporters marshalled on both sides.

In truth, they looked strange to any watchers who had not come across them before. They were dressed in many different styles, both men and women, wearing shirts and dresses, jeans and t-shirts, overalls and track suits. It was clear they represented many different walks of life. Yet, what made them special to look at was the fact that they all wore identical white balaclavas so that they looked like some crazy band of puppets from a children's cartoon, or the bad taste of a mushroom painting.

As soon as she joined, Genoveva discovered that the reason for this strange headgear was they wished to represent the nation as a whole, not themselves as individuals. They were members of a greater humanity, not just their own individual identities. That was the metaphorical power of their anonymity.

There were practical reasons, too. Because they were unpopular with the landowners, and because their message was dangerous to a government that wished to tell the people how to vote and behave, people who had spoken sympathetically about the EAS had been picked on, even though as yet no one had owned up to actual membership of the group. But even for the tacit supporters of the EAS, there had been inexplicable damage to cars and homes and businesses.

When workers thought they had been contracted for jobs, they found agreements suddenly withdrawn. Permission had been withheld for marches and demonstrations on more than one occasion. Each time they published a newsletter or held another gathering, tension crackled in the air. It was now an open secret that the governor of the state had asked for—and been given—extra powers to suppress insurrection when needed. Things were approaching a kind of climax. In such a situation, the leader said, anonymity is critical. Once they fix on one of us, once they feel strong enough to unmask us, both figuratively and literally, they can personalise our struggle and that will damage us. Once they move against one of us with their power we will be forced to defend that person and we will all be distracted.

This was the group Genoveva was hurrying to meet up with, despite her exhaustion. This is also why she was so alarmed by Dolores's comment. She neither wanted to face danger and inconvenience for herself nor cause unnecessary trouble to all the others. But she wanted to do something, to make a contribution, to say that *yes*, she had played her part in making the world a better place.

Rosario

TIA ROSARIO WIPED the residue of refried beans from around her daughter's lips. She reflected on the irony of having to look after a grown-up child when it should be the other way round. Of course, Marcelita was not really grown-up at all, despite her periods and full breasts, her hairy armpits and downy upper lip. She was simple-minded. That was the best and kindest way to describe her. She followed her mother around the crumbling hacienda on the hillside apparently contented, a look of infinite patience in her placid eyes, and nothing, Godammit, nothing (Rosario cursed) in her feeble brain.

I am an old woman now, she reflected bitterly as she took the plates to the stone sink for rinsing (because why should she spend money on a new kitchen when there was no point?). My almost middle-aged child-daughter should have given me a grandchild by now, a little boy, someone who would hold my hand and make me laugh, someone who would say yes, grandmother, and I love you, Grandmother.

What am I doing? she asked herself with sickening predictably, wiping the beginnings of tears away with the back of her wrist, the old litany of regret, blame, and love denied flooding her brain with its predictable monotony. Did she not love Marcelita? Of course she did. She is a gift from God, a sweet innocent, and are they not the most precious angels in His kingdom? Then she thought of her brother, old now and fading, and the life he had led with all its excitements and muscularity. She raked over his disappointment when his son Federico had rejected the charro life and had instead chosen to use his brain rather than his arms and thighs to squeeze some meaning from life.

She had resented her brother terribly for his disapproval. If only she had given birth to a Federico, she told herself, with his fight against authority, she would be a happy woman, even if he was not able to hold on to his own wife. Then she might have had a grand-child like—the thought of her grand-niece poured biliously into her gut and she was again suffused with jealousy. Everyone loved Angelita, the musician so much, but they only just managed to tolerate her own talentless child-woman daughter.

Stop it, stop it, Tia Rosario remonstrated, entwined in fronds of guilt and overcome with remorse. She was a good Christian woman. That is what she had always tried to be. Even if she could not stop her internal outpourings of envy, she was at least good enough to reproach herself for it.

It had not always been so. *My God*, she howled silently to the one being she could say anything to, who understood her, and who, as far as she could tell, did not judge her half so harshly as she judged herself. "My God why do you only give us one life so that we get old and only think of what might have been? How are we expected to live with the knowledge of our failures? Why have you given us the dubious gift of mortality if all we can do is think of things we have not done and regret things we ought not to have done?"

She turned to look at the back of her daughter's apparently empty head. "Why," she asked, keeping the channel to her deity open with yet more probing, "have you let us sail out into the deep lifeless lake of unrealised fulfilment? Oh God, the things I might have done, the places I might have seen. Yet you put my own brother in my way, made him the instrument of my undoing, of my incarceration, and though I know there is a purpose in everything you do, sometimes I think you must be a little careless—or perhaps it is that I am too stupid to appreciate your design."

She flinched at her own blasphemy, praying that she would be forgiven for her calamitous musings. Yet, what else was she to do in this silent house except think, scratch away at the scab of the past, send the ugly contemplation of dry sorrow round and round in the suffocating stillness of her empty life? *If only. If only.*

Marcelita suddenly stood up, knocking her chair backward, and shuffled off towards the bathroom. Tia Rosario had no choice but to follow her so that she could prevent the possibility of any accident.

If only she had not been forced to reject Don Venustiano's advances all those years ago. *If only.* As she helped her daughter in the performance and the aftermath of the most natural of bodily functions with a manual dexterity acquired from years of obligatory performance, her mind, all her senses, was elsewhere, at a long low cattle shed, swept and cleaned, hung with lanterns and paper flags, crisscrossed across rafters and walls. The smell of salsas bubbling in open *casuelas* seemed to her, even now, sweeter than anything she had ever managed to create for herself, and though she was known to be a good cook these days she rarely bothered. In that cattle shed, there had been violins and guitars, trumpets braying in the happy atmosphere, swirling bodies, and stamping feet. The whole town was there—or at least it seemed like that—for the first real celebration of Independence since before the revolution and the years of trouble and instability which followed its inconclusive resolution. Now, finally, there was a stable government, people were tired of plots and conspiracies and only wanted to live their lives in peace.

So, they sang and swayed, and as the midnight hour approached they danced right out of the shed, the musicians leading them, the stars their individual spotlights, until they reached the town hall, and there, on the balcony, frock-coated and sashed-up in the national colours, the mayor shouted out the patriotic words and they yelled back in a long-held refrain. Someone let off fireworks, great bangs echoing in the arched roof of the sky, and they all cheered. The world wrapped them round with its perfection. For Rosario, young and beautiful, high-breasted with her hair gathered up in curls, her long white skirts fluttering in the breeze, it was nothing short of miraculous.

As the explosions of happiness split the night, she looked over and saw the most handsome man she had ever been conscious of standing just below the balcony overhang. He leant against a pillar, one leather-booted ankle crossed lazily over another, his hands hooked into a wide scorpion-motif belt, a long-barrelled pistol strapped to his thigh, his eyes languid and bright in the flashing torchlights. As she watched, he pushed his wide-brimmed hat further back from his brow and reaching into a breast pocket, selected a small cigarillo which he lit with deliberate nonchalance. As she stood rooted to the ground beneath her by the imprisoning shackles of his beauty, he turned and looked at her so that she seemed to feel hands reach inside of her to pluck unknown muscle and sinew into quivering expectation.

She couldn't take her eyes off him, and the more she looked, the more he smiled back, his clipped moustache lining his resolute mouth. When, without conscious thought, she found herself standing before him she was incapable of sensible speech and quite unable to put together a rational thought. The man took off his hat, revealing thick immaculately parted hair, and announced that he was Venustiano Heredia. Before she had absorbed the name, he bent towards her and without asking for permission (since this was completely unnecessary), he placed his rich lips upon hers, transforming her silence into a crescendo of romantic ecstasy. When the kiss was over, so inordinately brief yet so profoundly everlasting, he asked her name and where she lived.

Oh, the sound his voice, she marvelled to herself as she hugged her night-gowned young body in the moonlight when they had returned to the hacienda. It was so melodious, so strong. Only later did she begin to wonder whether his attitude had changed when she told him who she was. Perhaps it was the arrival of her brother who approached them. Venustiano Heredia bowed, and ambled away round the corner of the building, taking her heart with him. He promised to call.

The contemplation of perfect bliss and unknown possibility—a jumble of secrets she could only guess at—enveloped her waking and dreaming thoughts all through the subsequent night as she tossed and turned with the extraordinary excitement of it all. But at breakfast the next day, incoherent with the hallucinations of the night before, her joy was cruelly terminated. When she came downstairs, she found her brother standing at the end of the room, his brooding silence heavy with menace. She had seen him like this before, especially after a good party such as last night's so she took little notice. She sat down and poured herself a coffee. But her brother, all puffed up and sombre with the responsibility he had been obliged to assume since his father's death the year before, came and stood by her side, arms behind his back. He started to speak to a place just above her head.

"That man," he announced. He did sound a little bit like their father.

"What man?" she replied as lightly as she could, as if her crazy soul was not singing with him, as if her body was not humming with promise.

"Heredia," he shot back. "That's who. That bastard Heredia." He stopped, waiting for a reply. She could think of nothing to say.

"How could you, *hermanita*? How could you?" he asked, exasperated by her young face twitching with emotion before him. "After our father. After everything."

Yes, yes, I know, she wanted to tell her brother, but by the time he had given her his name last night, she was already lost, already found. His kiss had dislocated her reason. A man that beautiful. So what if at every turn he and his family had held out against every reform the revolution had been fought for? So what if Heredia's father had betrayed a group of *campesinos* to the *federales* when they were hiding out in the barn adjoining the family mansion? So what if the Heredia family had been among the evil dictator's greatest supporters in those days? Venustiano, not much older than her own brother, had set Rosario aflame, her body's needs obliterating the brain's loyalties. But, her brother was forged in the furnace where revolutionary tales were minted, where recrimination for anti-revolutionists was still justifiable, and their downfall was passionately hoped for.

He did not hesitate. With the approval of the family and all their friends, he forbade her from seeing the object of her awakening ever again. When she protested, cried, and screamed at him, he locked her in her room, where she stayed for over a month. When he came to see her, he poured hatred and criticism into her ears, professing that he did it all for love.

During that time, she hardly ate, and her sleep was punctuated by nightmares and a terrible stabbing grief that kept her awake for hours. In the end, thin as the poorest peasant on the Heredia estate, her mind enfeebled by deprivation, her spirit cowed by forces too strong for her young optimism, she gave in to despair. Her brother knew that it was safe to let her out again. When she heard, six months later, that Venustiano Heredia had married the daughter of one of the other landowning families in the valley beyond San Miguel, she hardly felt a thing. She herself married a boring local pharmacist ten years later because she thought that she ought to. When he died at an early age during a nasty outbreak of cholera, she cried because everyone else did.

"At least," her brother said, "you have Marcelita."

She wanted to lash out at his patronising complacency. *You try having Marcelita*, she wanted to scream, *instead of that nice young Federico.* But she did not, because there seemed no point, and besides she was too tired.

If only. How would she have felt now, with her brother and everyone else she knew sympathetic to that band of crazies with their white balaclavas and their demonstrations? They were all doing their best to shame the caciques in the valleys. They reviled them, protested against them, chorusing their hatred and disapproval.

How would she feel now, she thought, as she adjusted Marcelita's clothes, if she was the Señora de Heredia, the old wife of the old man who headed that kingdom? What would she think if that old man stood at her side and she stood at his? Would she feel guilty? Would her conscience ruin her happiness? How would she be able to face her brother and his conscience-stricken son with the beautiful daughter?

Tia Rosario searched in her heart for a sense of rightness, for a path well-chosen, a life well-lived as she returned to the washing at the sink. She could not honestly say she would ever find it. At least, not before her remaining spirit was drowned in bitterness.

Alexei

ALEXEI KASSOLONIKI, he of the gaunt, bearded face, still thin and sinewed with elastic muscle despite the passage of time, found his breath shortening. For a moment, before he remembered the disaster of the previous day, he wondered if this presaged some future illness—emphysema, perhaps, or a heart attack. When he recalled the sense of disembodied emptiness he had felt as his hangover had drifted off yesterday, he reasoned that his physical limitations on this early sun-glazed morning had more to do with the after-effects of that, rather than being the result of any more general corporeal disintegration. Every step was more progress upward, after all, and it was already beginning to get hot.

The toxicity of all that alcohol, the dehydration he had suffered, all those things left their mark. Anyway, he told himself, aware that he was dropping behind the others, it is what is awaiting him that is so exciting. Who cares about a short spell of breathlessness? All around him, he could smell the odour of sulphur, an exotic garlic afterbreath. It is what is to come which concerns us, not any individual weakness or preoccupation.

He climbed on, once stopping to breathe deeply, angrily trying to fill his lungs with air. "I'm pathetic!" he said telepathically to his absent wife. "I just can't drink like I used to. I must be getting old."

The three scientists ahead of him had just passed the half-way mark up the cone of Artemio's Fire. They were ascending silently, purposefully, in a steady rhythm, and single file. Alexei resolved to follow their example, making sure that the distance between them did not grow. If he lengthened his stride, he might even catch up with them before they reached the top.

He started by matching the rhythm of his colleagues—one foot in front of the other and regular as a chronometer. He was careful where he put his heavy boots as he marched up the main trail. Even here, he could slip if he was careless, and none of them were real mountaineers.

Their skill was in measuring and gauging risk. Their training was in listening to the murmur of rocks, sifting the messages on the wind, feeling the ground beneath their feet, and calculating the pressure in the under-earth. Then there were the craters to study, great bowls of possibility and danger, where eyes drank fire and the nostrils were full of the scent of magic.

How they got onto their volcanoes and scrabbled up to their slavering mouths was only a means to an end. Of course, they tended to choose the safest routes, well-worn and reliable (unless they could hitch a helicopter ride), unlike their rock-climbing contemporaries to whom path-walking was to fingertip-holds as chairlifts are to a ladder climb. But they still had to be careful, Alexei knew. If they started fooling around, if they left the main path, hell, it was more dangerous than galloping up the stairs after a few too many drinks. But it wasn't his fault if suddenly bad judgement intervened. This wasn't his volcano. He didn't own it, wasn't responsible for its behaviour. No one was forced to come and see it. They made their own decisions.

The surface of Artemio's Fire was black and stony, occasionally loose underfoot. As he climbed he dislodged small pieces of volcanic rubble, more like dust, which he could foresee skittering down the steep slope with trails of residue behind them like earthy comets. He stopped to watch. Right down there at the bottom, a party of tourists, possibly girls, were just getting off the horses they probably hired to bring them this far. They would have passed the crumbling church tower of Tres Rios two kilometres away, still peering drunkenly above the black lava dust which had buried the rest of the village.

He observed the girls idly as they started their climb, hair flowing, and foolishly wearing trainers or even sandals. When his children had come to visit, he'd brought them proper boots, for once insisting on his decision against Vicky's pleading that surely it wasn't necessary, not just for one climb.

"Their feet grow so fast, when else will they ever use them?" she asked.

He'd stuck to his guns. Why then, when he tried to remember their climb, a long and happy day during which he had done his best to enthuse them with the same excitement that animated him, was the picture absent, the memory buried?

He started to climb again, but his rogue brain insisted on images he did not wish to view and which he hadn't actually seen himself, after all. His vision was once again dominated by the slipped footfall, the exclamation, laughter-like, the trip, and then the body turning over and over, rolling away down the steep slope. It was a children's game, round and round, the smile suddenly slack, stone instead of grass, the snap of limb, the crack of a temple, tumbling, tumbling down, on and on, the bottom never reached, never seen.

That had absolutely nothing to do with me, Alexei insisted to himself. A fluke. A terrible misfortune. Not my problem. Except the after-effects were. He tried to stop his knowledge nagging away at his consciousness so that he could concentrate on the movements they were tracking. He needed to read the secrets of the earth's entrails. He wanted to marvel at this black jewel set in the verdant plain. Artemio's Fire was an interloper, fascinating in its sheer waywardness.

Sweat poured from his face and neck. It moistened the curled hair of his beard, collecting in a pool where his collarbones met at the base of his throat. He wiped the sweat away and forced his thoughts from past tragedies to past experiences, from imagination to knowledge. In the past minor earthquakes, sudden eruptions of spite had sometimes been part of a continuing pattern of volcanic generation. On other occasions, they had been the first warning subjects of a cataclysmic symphony. That's when these huge forces, unstoppable, never propitiated, would bellow up out of the earth's core and he would be filled yet again with something greater than himself, something greater than his love and hate, something which humanity, with all its ingenuity and avariciousness, was incapable of doing anything about. We can build houses to be proof against typhoon and tempest. We can, if the money goes into construction rather than the constructor's pockets, make houses largely proof against earthquakes. Big ships can ride out monstrous waves. Aeroplanes can be designed to absorb the roughest turbulence. But there is nothing, Alexei would tell anyone, any civilian who would listen, absolutely nothing you can do about a volcano when it blows. It doesn't matter if it's on some remote archipelago or hovering over the biggest city in the world, dormant way back into the mists of recorded and remembered time. When Tlacoltepeca sees that young man wrap his enfolding arms around his daughter, he just lets rip, mindless of ant-like humanity or any other living thing.

Confused humans are driven to find some explanation for it, so they invent gods and demons, talk about divinity, and try to bend the uncontrollable wrack of nature to some manageable level. But once they have experienced pyroclastic flow, the billowing clouds of poisonous bile racing out of the ruptured skin of a jagged peak, once they have seen the epic scale of such velocity as it cuts off the life of every living thing for miles around, gods are irrelevant and humanity is nothing more than an afterthought. There is something so awe-inspiring about this, so all-embracing, like the surrender of self into the greatest music, the abandonment of the strongest passion, the sickliest embrace of the most final consummation, that Alexei, like many of his fellow obsessives, was constantly pulled into the path of destruction. It is like the smallest flying thing being impelled to flame and die in the flicker of seduction. It was the thing itself, the sheer savage joy of it, that he craved.

From the top of Artemio's Fire, the verdant valleys to the south of San Miguel stretched away into the hazy distance. To the north was the town itself, still too small for cityhood, but growing almost daily. The classical harmony of its central square with the *portales* where Migueleños sat to eat and drink was being drowned out by the noises of disorganised suburbia. To the west and east, the chains of hills and peaks, friendly vertebrae, held the country's muscled torso together as one functioning organism. Around the scientists, as they looked down into the crater rim, was the black aridity, planet-like, of volcanic despoliation, the dried rock and dust still too young for the growth of living things. It was this lunar landscape, together with the irresistible romanticism of the volcano's comparative youth, that drew people to the area. A climb up Artemio's Fire was a necessary activity on the backpackers' lists of things to be done. The contemplation of the mountain's bleak slopes produced a thousand different photographs every week.

Now, with the imminence of the festival which the Migueleños had dreamed up as a way of bringing an even larger number of people to the area, the scuffed dome of the mountain's construction would be more visited, discussed, and trampled on than ever. There were going to be concerts, parades, special readings, civic events, speeches, and non-stop television coverage.

If anyone had suggested that Alexei would get involved with such a thing, that he would find the actions of a small group of people interesting or worth dealing with, he would have laughed at them. That was before he came to this place and found himself suddenly affected by something genuine, real, sweet, and gentle. There were people he thought he could trust. Not the festival, but what they might do at the festival—if only someone could think of something.

He returned his thoughts to the earth's acned exterior, the new fumaroles on the mountainside. Then he felt it, that deep excitement in his gut as he stood looking down into the crater he had just climbed and assessed its lava dome. They don't have to worry. Artemio's Fire will not let them down. For if he was not mistaken, it's got a show of its own all lined up and ready to go.

Don Venustiano

DON VENUSTIANO HEREDIA was conscious of his discomfort with every laboured step he took along the echoing corridor on the first floor of City Hall. He was not about to let anyone else know how he was feeling, though. He was a proud man, unprepared to show any weakness on the face or his unstoppable ageing. Eve worse in his case, some burnt-out blood vessels in his brain had malfunctioned, provoking a stroke that had left him furiously angry and, for a time, scared witless in a private room of the best hospital in the state. He'd lost the movement on his left side. His left leg and arm were suddenly heavy and useless, hanging from his torso, determined to unbalance him, whether he lay, sat, or stood.

He'd fought it as a man should, fiercely appropriating every glimmer of returning sensation, sternly abjuring every neuron and synaptic connection he could find to take over functions now permanently lost to those parts of his brain that had been inciner-ated in the attack. He had never been defeated by anyone or anything, and although he supposed he would have to die, one day, like everyone else, he would do it as a man of action, not as some craven invalid, spittoon in hand, hip-quivering, and senile.

So here he was, barely able to jerk his heavy leg forwards toward the office of the Alcalde, San Miguel's mayor. He was the most powerful official in the state after the governor. Don Venustiano was determined to get something done. Someone had to put a stop to all this, to nip it in the bud.

In the first outer office, the secretary tried to delay him. "But sir," he wavered unhappily. "Do you have an appointment?" He obviously did not know who he was talking to. Don Venustiano simply marched on, and when the young man rose to head him off, he used his good arm to push him back into his seat.

At his cries of "Señor, Señor, you cannot pass," a security guard came running in from outside. Unbuttoning the leather holster at his belt, he began to remove his pistol that crouched there.

The old man must have been aware of this. In the doorway that led into the next office, he turned, and fixing the frightened guard with a rheumy malevolence, told him not to be so stupid. "Go back to your post and stop dangerous people from getting in," he barked, and his imperative was so commanding that the guard's hand fell limply. He shuffled back out of the room.

In the next office, two pretty young women looked up from computer screens and seeing a sclerotic old man stumping towards them, made to get up (in one case) and dial for help (in the other). They need not have bothered. Ignoring them and the four supplicants who were waiting for their mayoral interview, Don Venustiano swayed unstoppably through the next doorway until he found himself in the third waiting room, the final gateway to the seat of power.

He recognised a man sitting on the sofa to his right. He was formally attired and clutching a briefcase. Sweat moistened his upper lip. He was the rector of the university of San Miguel. A woman, older and appearing prosperous, was unknown to him. The woman behind the kidney-shaped desk was an old acquaintance of his, however. She was a feisty battle-axe called Aurora Melia, a *soltera* bound to her infirm mother, who had nursed a secret devotion to the mayor for years. This was safe because it was unlikely ever to be consummated. It was this, however sad, that made it perfectly appropriate for the faithful secretary.

"Don Venustiano!" she said in surprise. "I was not expecting to see you today. I do not seem…" She flicked the pages of a diary over in her confusion. "…to have you in El Señor Alcalde's list of appointments for today."

"Bugger appointments," the landowner snapped back, barely pausing in his onward march. "Is he in there?"

"Well yes, but he's got some people in there with him. Don Venustiano, please sir." She stepped out from behind her desk, and despite her plumpness, moved with speed to head him off. He got there before her, turning the ornate handle before wrenching open the door and propelling himself into the room beyond.

The Alcalde, Silvestre Ocampo, was seated in his designated armchair at the head of a small circle of two women and a man. They all looked up at his precipitate entrance.

"Don Venustiano," the mayor said, his suaveness having to work hard to mask his consternation. "How nice to see you. This is a surprise."

"Bugger that!" snapped his uncompromising visitor. "We need to talk."

"Of course," the mayor replied. "I'm sure I can find some time later on. If you'd like to talk to Aurora…"

"Now!" the visitor snapped.

"Well, that's a bit difficult old friend. You see, because we're having a meeting, you see, about the festival. It's getting pretty close."

"That's just too bad, because you and I need to talk. Now, since I am here, would seem to be a pretty good time to do it."

"Come on, Don Venustiano, you're being a bit unreasonable."

"Don't 'Don Venustiano' me, you bastard. I've come here to talk to you on a matter of some urgency. Get rid of these people—they can wait outside—and we can get down to it."

The mayor was at a loss. People did not normally speak to him this way, least of all here in his office, in front of others. But then, Venustiano Heredia was not just anybody. If Silvestre Ocampo called security and had him thrown out, there would be a terrible row, which in the end, he would probably lose. On the other hand, he couldn't ask the others to leave. That would involve a complete loss of face after the manner in which the old man had talked to him. What was he to do? He stood there indecisively, his mind racing, and silently cursing the landowner for putting him in this position. He could feel that he was going red.

In the end, it was one of the women who saved him. She was from the organising committee, and he fancied her a bit. What was her name? Marisol, that was it, Marisol Cordova. She was sweet.

"Señor Alcalde," she smiled, "there are still matters which I and my fellow committee members have to discuss. I wonder if there is a room somewhere that we could use for a little meeting, say, for about half an hour? Then, we can come back and continue our conversation with you."

He could have kissed her, would like to have kissed her, in fact. Instead, he called Aurora Melia and asked her to take his visitors to the conference room down the corridor. It was too big for their purposes, but it was the best he could come up with on the spur of the moment.

The door closed. He was alone with the old man from the valley.

"Now then, Don Venustiano, what can I do for you? What is so important that you honour me with your presence in this manner?" He could feel the muscles which controlled his jawbone tightening with anger. It was making itself felt now that the others had gone.

"I want to know what you're going to do about that bunch of crazies, left-wing idiots, those communists."

"I'm sorry, who? Who do you mean exactly?" He knew perfectly well, of course, but he needed the advantage of stalling. "Wouldn't you like to sit down?"

"No, dammit, I'm fine standing. You know perfectly well who I mean. The 'Ejercito de Arturo Sanchez', or whatever they call themselves, that's who."

"I think this is a matter for the state governor. It is surely not something to be considered by this humble servant," Silvestre countered egregiously, saying anything he could think of to get the man off his back.

"Well, that's where you're wrong Mister Mayor. You're in control of the city police, and you're in charge of your own streets. It's your call, don't you think?"

"Well, perhaps I am, but what exactly would you have me do?

This is a democracy. The people have a right to make their opinions heard. That's what our revolution was all about, if you recall."

"Son of a bitch! Are you trying to make fun of me? Are you daring to treat this as some kind of a joke? Are you? Because if you are, so help me God, I'll…"

"Don Venustiano, calm yourself. I assure you I meant no disrespect. Now then, what is it exactly that you think my office can help with?"

"It's this stupid festival of yours, the volcano thing. I've heard they're planning a big demonstration in the middle of it. There's even talk of them coming onto our land with their insolent chants, their ridiculous demands, and those stupid bastard hoods. I want you to have the whole thing stopped, that's what. Banned. You and the governor. Because if not, I'll have to send my own men into town, and I do not want to do that."

"If I didn't know you better, Don Venustiano, I'd say that you were threatening me."

"You're damn right I am. Seems you know me just fine."

"Well sir, frankly that isn't necessary. We are perfectly aware of that group's stratagems. We have made contingency plans in case the demonstration goes ahead, but frankly, we are not too worried. We have found a way of infiltrating the group. In short, your worries may soon be over."

"They'd better be, that is, if your party wants to count on our future support, or if you want us to keep on bankrolling you so you can bribe all those poor suckers to vote for you every time you have what you laughingly call a democratic election. Bunch of hypocrites. This thing had better be resolved fast. Our support comes at a price, let me remind you."

Don't I know it, the mayor said to himself. He wished it was otherwise so he could kick Don Venustiano out of his office, the arrogant old shit. Hell, he didn't start the system rolling. He didn't manufacture the web that binds them to the wealthy and the venal. They just have to work within it, that's all because he doesn't (he pushed away the familiar guilt) have the guts to do anything about it.

"How's that charming young daughter of yours?" he asked in his silkiest voice. He meant, of course, the young girl Don Venustiano had fathered with his mistress twenty years ago. She was now suing him in a case that the newspapers loved, even though he was doing his best to shut them up.

The old man's eyes nearly shot out of his head as anger rushed through him. "That's none of your damn business…" he stopped, forcing an iron control to stop himself exploding with rage.

He was not going to lose face in front of this man, this political whore. He only tolerated him because he and his friends needed the complicity of politicians if they were to hold onto what was rightfully theirs. Besides, he was feeling suddenly tired. He feared a return of the dizziness he had experienced on more than one occasion since his attack. He needed to get out of there and back to the limousine waiting for him downstairs. It was time to finish this meeting.

"Do we have an agreement? No demonstration during the festival, right? You people have to stop it or else we will. Do we understand each other?"

"Perfectly, Don Venustiano. We understand each other very well."

Later, when the old man had dragged himself away, the mayor chuckled at his own audacity. He was pleased at the way he had turned the tables on his visitor. But later still, as his chauffeur drove him home through the evening traffic, he thought about their meeting again. What was he to do about the EAS with the whole world watching? How could he suppress them without ruining San Miguel's reputation and bringing calumny upon himself?

The movement had to be stopped. The system made it unavoidable. The question was how.

The Twins

THIS NEW PLACE WAS STRANGE, noisy, and unclean. What they could see through the tinted windows filled them with disquiet. But of course, they no longer had anything to fear. They had moved on to a higher plane, more pure of spirit than ever before, and purged of the filthy mess that the mass of people who lived in perpetual darkness seemed to be unaware of.

They still had a long way to go, of course, and many more awesome challenges to surmount before they could dream of Full Luminescence. Indeed, there was no absolute guarantee that they would ever get there. Many were still trapped at the stage of Illumination, after all, and might never rise higher. However, the twins had suffered all the necessary pains and become more and more quiescent, so that the Halo, their spiritual leader, their almost God, had passed them through the six stages of Celestial Lightening. Their path was now clear.

It had not been easy. From the moment that they had decided independently to leave their lives behind them (but we are never independent, the Halo told them at every lights-out preamble, we are only the servants of a greater lightening), and step out of the darkness, their existence had been a series of trials and tribulations, temptations to be resisted, and tasks to perform. Sometimes, now, they forgot what it was that made them join, except that what lay behind them was fearful and onerous. What lay ahead was light and perfect.

The very first tasks they set were all directed towards leaving the past where it belonged—in the dark. That was why they were denied sleep for their first week, goaded and supported by a team of Lighteners who took turns to shout them to wakefulness or drag them to the cold purity of the Ice Tank when their flagging neurons needed enervation. Like all novice Lighteners, they were allowed to drink wholesome draughts of unsweetened black coffee, a beverage forbidden to all except those undergoing the First Trial. They were undressed and washed ritually five times every day and five times every night. Worst of all, they were kept in separate rooms, and though they both knew how the other was feeling, because they were each feeling it himself, they would have found the whole drawn-out cycle of terrifying deprivation easier to bear if they had been in each other's company.

The Halo knew how to prepare followers for lightening: one week of no sleep, no sleep at all, the obliteration of any but the most primitive and jagged thoughts, and the strange cold ritual of washing and immersion. This was all designed to shift personalities out of their normal orbits and break their characters down into hallucinating sponges, new and absorbent, ready for the truth. Even before the Scourging, an impenetrable barrier had been thrown across the road leading back to the past.

At the end of the Sleepless Week, the brothers were shriven and shaved, all the hair from their bodies cleaned away, plucked even from their crevices and secret places. When they had been given the plain shapeless garments that all the Sons of Perpetual Light wore, they were taken before the Halo, purified and whole, as the book said. Following instructions, they abased themselves before him, facing away from him, their backmost points raised impossibly high (symbolic of the Gathering), their faces pressed to the floor. When their robes were raised and knotted rope lashed across their bare skin, they showed little reaction except for a twitch of their thighs as the ropes whistled towards them each time. Only the unmistakable intake of breath told the ecstatic watchers how much control the new initiates were being forced to exercise. The older ones among them remembered a time before their own Banishment of the Dark; the younger ones were suddenly conscious of painfully glorious memories and seemed to feel their own skin blister and bleed under their hanging costumes.

New initiates wore their first tunics for two weeks following the Scourging for the Banishment of the Dark. The blood stains were regarded as a mark of honour, and were eagerly looked for as a sign of celestial acceptance. Whenever the Halo passed and they bowed deeply away from him, like all who had not yet reached full Enlightenment, he would say, "Ah, so you still carry the sign of the Beginning." They should answer, "Yes, Halo, truly the Darkness is past," and would be grateful for his attention. When, finally, they swapped their blood-stained tunics for the regular ones, they treasured their stigmatised garments like old wedding dresses.

Some time later, they completed the Trial of the City, walking through the poisoned lung of the metropolis, to demonstrate that they were strong enough to withstand its dangerous obscurity. They would not be dragged down into its lifeless depths. It was the first time the twins had been back since they had gone to live at Halo Centre (a large hacienda, walled and guarded at all times, bare and quiet except for His quarters which were full of equipment he himself was obliged to maintain to stay in contact with the outside world; only the Halo and those who had reached full luminescence were thought able to resist the deadly viruses which such contact exposed them to). That is why a van followed behind them as they chorused down the street ready, at the slightest provocation, to rescue any of them who were still vulnerable.

It was a good thing the vehicle was there because suddenly, as they made their journey, a Dark couple started shouting and waving from a car. They were about to come after them. Star, a Luminescent, saw the look on the twins' faces, a mixture of memory, guilt, revulsion, and need, all the things that Sons of Perpetual Light were at risk from when confronted with their past, and the group was in the van on the road home before they could even recite the Canticle of Belonging.

There was the Test of the Spirit Weakening, when lined up

outside the main building just as dawn was insinuating its mischievous fingers through the towers and railings, they were made to remove their shifts and stand, shivering in the damp coolness of the morning. The twins thought (to each other) how beautiful, how ecstatic it was for the Sons of Perpetual Light to partake of such a wonder in such a pure and natural state, their shaved heads and bodies raw and cleansed.

But then, to their horror, they saw figures approaching from the Halo's own Lightquarters. As they came closer, the young men realised that they too were naked. Instead of the sandpapered acquiescence of male bodies they were used to, these were round women, rolled curves of skin and hair growth ever more evident as the sky grew lighter and the intruders came upon them.

"Stand," the Halo's voice said, "and make the Test of the Spirit weakening." So they stood, ten of them, young and at some level, wretched and afraid. The women rubbed their flesh against them and stroked with warm and pliant hands the parts that should never be touched by any from the Darkness nor any from the Light except for the Gathering. What was now happening was a horror unimaginable and unpardonable.

The Halo had watched with three Luminescents at his side. They held the familiar knotted ropes, bloodied from many Banishments. When one of the twins, weak, ashamed, and spiritually upset by the importuning of the woman's expert fondling, nevertheless felt himself responding to the first touch upon him for a great length of time, and sensed the unstoppable blood flow, he knew what was coming.

Abandoned now by the sluttish temptress, his weakness standing out from him for all to see, he was set upon by the Luminescents, their ropes thrashing down upon his chest, thighs, legs, shoulders, buttocks, and torso. It was terrifying, shaming, and utterly disgusting. When he fell to his knees in abasement, he knew that he had failed. He felt the danger of Darkness ever more keenly than the scourging of the physical abuse that rained down upon him.

He was joined by his brother and then by three of the others, young, impressionable, and easily aroused in the early morning, even in the most improbable circumstances, but now retching and freshly detumescent in the agony of their humiliation. They stayed there, bleeding, unclothed, and fearfully exposed while all the Sons of Perpetual Light came to witness their pain.

"Sons," boomed the Halo's voice, "this is the Test of The Spirit Weakening one of the most difficult tests of all. Five of you have failed the test and must be re-proofed before you may be advanced. For is it not the Halo's Law that even though we are sons of Darkness, a thing we cannot now undo, we abjure the luscious temptations of excitement which are dark and sinful? Is it not a chief pillar of our belief that we banish entire from our world the needs of the body, making it a passive home for our inner enlightenment? Sons, remember who we are and what we do upon this earth. We gather strength from the Purity of Light, not from the excreta of Darkness. When we achieve Luminescence we are then ready and able to take our place in the cleanness of all spirituality, and then, only then, can we move our attention out to the stellar spaces where the Light, the only Light, is allowed to purify us all and where we will live, spirits only, for all eternity.

"And we do wish to live for all eternity, do we not?"

There was a murmur of approval.

"One eternity, one being with the stars, free from the sustenance and temptation of this woman earth?"

"Yes,' they cried, "that is what we want," as they dreamt of the spectral joy awaiting them, all spirit, all shriven and redeemed.

Both twins failed the next Test of the Spirit Weakening and were repeatedly beaten and humiliated. Then, one survived the temptation of arousal but had to watch his brother being reviled and chastised again. Only at the fourth test were both finally free.

Now, the Halo told them all one evening at Meeting, the volcano at San Miguel had passed fifty years since it first splattered its eructation over the countryside. This was a propitious moment for the Gathering, essence purified in volcanic fire.

There was a gasp, a long sigh, and in the days and weeks that followed the Sons of Perpetual Light shone a little bit brighter, terrified but ecstatic at the prospect of such a climactic celestial trial, ejaculatory and intimate, the spirit, just once, made flesh.

Genoveva

WHEN GENOVEVA DELGADILLO ACEVES arrived at the house on the Calle 14 de Abril, she went through the normal procedures for concealment. First, she walked around the block one way, and then another, stopping at a kiosk to buy the spicy powdered sweets she had enjoyed since childhood. This purchase allowed her to look all around and make sure that she was not being watched. Satisfied that she was not observed, she walked to the entrance of the *peña* where every night tourists sat in a semi-circle of tables to hear musicians play typical folk tunes while young dancers costumed appropriately for each dance swayed their fluid patterns in imitation of earlier times and practices.

As usual for this time of day, there was no one in sight as she walked through the entrance. Then, after turning left, she made her way along the corridor that ran down the side of the building. As she did so, she reached into her bag to remove the white hood that she pulled reluctantly over her freshly washed and brushed hair. At the end of the corridor, she reached the metal gate and pressed the buzzer.

"The hero?" barked a tinny voice from the speaker located to the right of the lock.

"The hero is Arturo Sanchez, as everyone should know."

"Number?"

"Forty-three."

With a click, the door unlocked itself and she pushed the iron railings inward. She knew the way by heart and so, with barely a pause in her stride, she pulled the door shut behind her and walked into a small courtyard behind the area they used for the restaurant and singing, which was hidden by plants and screens. There was a door on the left. She knocked, using the special rhythm they had all learned (the opening of the chorus of 'La Rebelde'). The door opened and she walked in.

Genoveva felt immediately ridiculous since none of the people sitting around the battered old table in the middle of the room were wearing hoods like the one that she had put on. For the first time since she had started coming here, they were all exposed. Even as she pulled the white balaclava from her own head (and fought, in a reflex action, to return her thick hair to its earlier lustrous shape), she was reeling in shock at the sight not only of one of the hospital consultants where she worked, but also of one of her best friends who had once dated Julio. They had all looked up as she came in and smiled as she stuffed the white wool back into her bag.

"Welcome," a tall man said. He had intense luminous eyes. She recognised him instantly from his voice as number 22, though she had never seen his face before. "Come in and join us. Please don't be surprised by the lack of disguise. It suddenly seemed silly for us not to know each other." He indicated a gaunt foreign-looking man with a heavy beard. "Alexei refused to wear a balaclava, so we all followed his lead. Of course, this doesn't mean that we're suddenly going to tell the whole world who we are—only that we may as well stop being so cloak-and-dagger about it when we're here. Does that make sense?"

"¡Hola Geny!" her friend Raquel said. Genoveva blushed and sat in the chair indicated by Doctor Martinez. Doctor Martinez? Not possible, surely. He worked at the hospital. Everyone was a bit scared of Dr Martinez.

"Hello, Nurse Delgadillo," he said, his smile icy.

Normally, members of the EAS introduced each other by number only—the number they had all been given when they first joined the movement. This was after an interview conducted by three hooded figures asking questions about the candidate's background and motivation. Genoveva had submitted herself to this uncomfortable ordeal (masked, as instructed in a notice pinned to the door of the interview room) after going to that first demonstration (for her) and picking up a leaflet. This leaflet instructed interested people to phone one of three numbers.

When she had done so, a voice at the other end of the line had subjected her to a series of grilling questions, some of which she could not see the point of. However, she must have answered satisfactorily, because at the end of the conversation, she had been given a different number to ring two days later.

Once again, she had been subjected to a bizarre and apparently directionless series of inquiries, and once again, she was given another number to contact. She only got to the interview after two more calls. Finally, when it was all over, she was given the number 43, and was integrated into the group. She did telephone interviewing herself now, attended meetings at the *peña*, helped to distribute publicity, and went on all their marches and demonstrations.

"We were just discussing," number 22 said, "what we are going to do during the celebrations to mark the fiftieth anniversary of the appearance of Artemio's Fire. It will be our best chance for publicity yet. There will be media from all over the world. If we play our cards right, we can get maximum exposure and make the whole world aware of the appalling conditions of the *campesinos* in the valleys. We can bring the corruption that allows this situation to continue to everyone's attention."

"I shouldn't think anyone's in much doubt about that, thanks to us," Dr Martinez said.

"I don't know about that," number 22 countered, "but this event, or whatever it is, provides us with an opportunity to reach right over the heads of the people we are protesting about. What I need from all of you is suggestions about how we can exploit this for our maximum advantage."

"They're not going to like it, of course," the bearded foreigner said.

"No, of course they won't. I still don't understand why they haven't acted before in any big way. But I suppose we have to realise that they'll have a real go at us if we look like disrupting any of the celebrations."

"Not if we plan it right," Genoveva found herself saying back to number 22, much to her own surprise.

"In what way?" a woman to her right said.

"Well, if lots of TV crews are there, with people watching even before we start doing, well, I don't know, whatever we are going to do, then the authorities or whoever are hardly going to charge in and start arresting us, are they? Or at least if they do, they're not going to beat us up or shoot us."

"I wouldn't be too sure of that!," the other woman said. "Look what happened to those students in the capital last year. They attacked them right in front of the tourists. We all saw the pictures on TV that first day."

"Yeah, and then the government fixed it so they didn't show the pictures again," Genoveva's friend chimed in.

"Surely, therefore," the foreigner in his deep accented voice added, "you… that is, *we* have to take steps to see that the authorities will find tolerating us less uncomfortable than putting a stop to any of our activities, with or without their guns and water canon."

"That all depends on what we want to achieve, doesn't it?" the older man at the other end of the table said.

"Good point," number 22 said, respectfully. Genoveva wondered who the older man was. "What exactly should our purpose be?"

"The same as always, I think," Raquel answered him. Genoveva had never realised how strong she was. "We want the largest number of people possible to realise what is going on. We want to create such an eruption of embarrassment that the authorities will have no choice but to act. We want to shame them into action with our power, the power of the people to order and direct."

The room seemed to echo with her stirring words. There was a silence, then, while they all tried to think of how to match them.

The older man was the first to say, quietly, "It'll take a lot to shame that crowd—look at that governor in the south. The whole world knew he was in with the drug barons but nobody lifted a voice —let alone a finger—against him."

"Hey, hold on," Doctor Martinez said. "That's just defeatist talk. You might as well pack up and go home if that's how you feel. I'm sorry sir, I don't mean to be disrespectful.

"Well no, you're quite right, I am sure," the older man replied meekly.

Genoveva was still feeling stupid about having walked into the room with her hood on. Even as she listened to the conversation developing around her, she found herself blushing at how clumsy and conspicuous she had looked, how she had stood out so gauchely.

"Hey," she said suddenly, blushing even more vehemently but feeling impelled by the force of the ideas that were cascading over her. "What we need to do is something visible, isn't that right? But if we plan demonstrations and marches they'll surround us, or they'll forcibly direct us away from the cameras, and the people. Somehow, we've got to resist that. We've got to be right in the middle of everything, someplace where everyone can't help seeing us, where they'll all find themselves taking us in. What I want to say is that suddenly, instead of looking at what they thought they were looking at, they'll find that all they can see is us. Does that sound sensible? I'm not quite sure how it would work, of course. Just a vague idea."

"Sounds very sensible indeed," number 22 said, smiling at her encouragingly, his eyes flashing with energy. "Let's follow that thought through. Being right in the middle of it. Being the thing that everyone is looking at. So let's think about what the big events are and then we can work out how to infiltrate them."

"The parade," the older man said. "The one that starts the whole thing off on Saturday. If we could get into that parade, perhaps."

"And the opening concert," Genoveva remembered. "The night before. Just think…" She was enjoying herself now, even as light-headed as she was from lack of sleep, and flushed with her knowledge of the approval that everyone in the room seemed to feel for her. "The auditorium is packed. Everyone is there, all the so-called distinguished guests, the foreigners, the journalists. Then, right in the still centre, perhaps the moment when the conductor lifts his conductor's stick, that's when we could do it."

"Do what?" the doctor asked, an eyebrow raised.

"Well suddenly, in that silence, people dotted around the audience stand up, that's us I mean with our balaclavas on, and we are so conspicuous. I know how I felt when I came in this morning."

She could feel herself blushing redder and redder now, but she went on as the picture became clearer in her mind. "And people look at us and they are embarrassed, unsure about what's going on, and the musicians see us and are distracted so the music starts in a ragged kind of way. But we just stand there in silence while the music plays on. Maybe the conductor looks round because he senses the strangeness in the air behind him. But we just stand and stand and stand until, in a break in the music, the end of a movement if they are playing a symphony or something like that, we make our way along the rows while everyone watches and some complain, and we walk down the aisles until we stand, all of us, in a line in front of the stage and we link arms, we bow, and finally, using the centre aisle only, we file out of the hall leaving everybody, performers and audience alike speechless and amazed. After that everyone will be talking about nothing else. They'll be talking about us and what we stand for. I'm sure they will."

"And so am I," number 22 said. "That sounds absolutely fantastic as a starter, and then we do something similar in the parade."

"Yeah," Raquel said. "we could try to mingle with the marchers, or even get our own little group together and simply join in so that the only way the police could prevent us would involve them in disrupting the whole parade."

"So let me get this right," the older man said. "We sit there and then we put on our hoods while we are sitting in the audience?"

"Well yes."

"All right. Yes. I think it can be done. What are they playing? Does anybody know?"

"I heard," the doctor said, looking across at the nurse, that there has been a cancellation. Now nobody's quite sure who's going to be on that stage."

"I had heard something of the same," number 22 said. "We just have to keep ourselves informed about that. But in the meantime, if we decide to go ahead with this woman's plans we will need to find out how many of us are going to be involved and how we can make sure that we get tickets."

"That will be no problem," the older man said. "I can guarantee a number of seats if you tell me soon how many we will require."

Genoveva looked at all the people around her, at the man known as 22 with his fine face and dancing eyes, at the gaunt foreigner, at the older man, and all the others. She smiled at Raquel and saw in her friend's gaze that she had done well with her suggestions and that she was among equals. As the tiredness washed around her brain, wavelike and choppy, she felt strong, happy, and purposeful.

This festival is just the beginning for me, she thought.

Part Three

The Long Drive North

Victoria

"Sorry, what was that?" Vicky said. The studio seemed hotter than usual and her ears were burning up beneath her headphones. She wished she had washed her hair that morning. Through the window she saw Sonja, her producer, gesturing at her in surprise. That's because (she told herself) the one thing I never do—I'm renowned for it—is lose the thread of what people are saying.

She had lost the thread this time, though. Lost it completely. For a timeless hole of a second, she had been completely unaware of where she was or what anyone was talking about. The fact that it was hardly surprising didn't make it any better. Her whole life was under attack from almost every direction. Maria was cowering in the house experiencing alternating bouts of bravery and terror. Martin was offended with her and was now talking about some masochistic visit to that volcano at San Miguel—and God knows what that would do to him. The children both looked as if they were about to come down with yet another respiratory infection and on top of all of this there was something wrong with Alex and she didn't know what.

He had rung her last night just after the children had gone to bed. The insistent ring of the phone had been a relief. It meant that she could legitimately leave the kitchen where she had been having a patchy conversation with Maria and move to the living room. The trouble was that for someone who made her living from talking, she could think of little to say to the maid. She had expressed sympathy, empathised, and cosseted the frightened woman for the last few days.

On two occasions when the door buzzer had sounded, it had been her and not Maria who had gone to the gate to find Juan standing there, looking forlorn and desperate so that she had to remind herself what kind of a person he was to stop her resolve from weakening. Both times she told him, dispassionately, that his wife did not wish to see him and that she, her employer, was minded to respect that wish. On the second occasion, he had started to protest, but she had used her foreign haughtiness to silence him. Still, the situation was unlikely to remain like this. If everything Maria had told her was true, he would be back.

Although, in her professional life, Vicky was happy to involve herself in the lives of others, handing out advice to all who rang into her radio phone-in programme for foreigners, she was less easy about becoming enmeshed in the real day-to-day lives of the people around her unless, of course, they were close friends or family. Just as the microphone and the headphones created a screen for her to hide behind, so she preferred to keep at least a symbolic distance between herself and the people who worked in the neighbouring *tiendas*, staffed the radio station, or, especially, worked for her in the house.

Before this last emergency, therefore, her conversations with Maria had been friendly and cheerful; they had discussed the traffic and the children, the weather and the unreliability of workmen, but nothing more. Now, though her instinct urged her to stand clear, she had no option but to take sides. That first night, for example, there had been no alternative but to get involved. Maria had been far beyond distance and politeness. Her misery had been so overpowering that the details of her personal life, intimate and shocking, poured out of her in a molten stream and Vicky was both personally moved and morally outraged by the plight of the distraught woman in front of her.

Now, however, they were both somehow ashamed of that intimacy since it had violated custom in such a marked way. Neither of them quite knew how to carry on from here: should they use the patterns of the past or the discourse of surrender, so recently exhibited? That is why, sometimes, there were awkward silences while they both wondered what the future was going to be like and what, if anything, they should say about it. Alexei's call, last night, had interrupted just such a moment.

"Vicky."

"Alexei, my love, hello. How are you?"

"Things are interesting, the future awaits us. OK, I suppose."

"Well, it's a bit tense here. Maria's husband has been to the house and I've had to tell him to go away. All a bit difficult really."

"Yes. I can imagine."

"And Maria, well—I mustn't speak too loud even if she doesn't understand, well, maybe she does—anyway, the kids have been asking questions, you know, and I think she feels kind of ashamed, and that's part of the unfairness of being hit by your husband. Well... Alexei, are you still there?"

"Yes, of course."

"So it's a bit strange round here at the moment."

"The world is full of injustice."

She was used to the distance in his voice when he was looking into the far-off spaces of the world. But these words were strange and insubstantial.

"So anyway, darling, what of you? How are you? How long are you going to be playing with that mountain? When are you coming back?"

"It has begun, Vicky. It has begun."

"What has begun?"

"The old gods are angry."

"Oh come on. What old gods? Who's angry? Alex this isn't like you."

"Yes. It's difficult to explain, I suppose. I mean I don't know how to explain it. Except the fire, the coming fire. You can feel it, the shaking earth, the crying out for change. There are good people here, bad people too. I tell you Vicky, it has begun."

"I'm sorry to be stupid, Alexei, love, but honestly I haven't the slightest idea what you are talking about."

Into her mind, unasked for, comes a vision of her husband being taken away from her on some rugged mountainside. But by what? It is not the engulfing smoke carpet of malevolence that he has told her about and about which she has so often been preoccupied. It is not even the hot stench of sulphurous detritus. Something else, a beckoning finger, a power stronger than her own, perhaps. The old gods? Don't be silly. But something wasn't quite right.

"The old power is waning, you see, and it must be diminished. And it will all come to pass when the volcano blows its top while the people celebrate and the earth's anger rips the future into a thousand pieces. That's what I mean."

"Oh please! Alexei, you're a scientist for God's sake. You're talking like a crazy man Alex?"

"We're all crazy now."

How stupid of her not to have heard it before. The slurring of the voice, the portentousness of the words.

"You've been drinking!"

"Well yes. Do you know Vicky it's really not my fault about that girl, Margarita, you know, Martin's girl. Not my fault. Not my fault at all."

"Of course it's not your fault. You weren't even there. How could it be your fault?"

"Yes, well. We all have to atone."

"Alex? Alex? What's got into you? What's going on? What is all this?"

"All this? All this? Oh Vicky, I'm sorry, I'm so sorry. I've had a bit too much to drink, that's all. I've been out with some new friends. Had a bit too much. Sorry."

"Who are they, this new crowd?"

"Ah, no. I'd better not say too much. You never know. Just people. Trying to make things better. Which they should be. Of course they should be. But who knows if there's time, what time there is. Artemio's Fire. Hah!"

He said goodbye and hung up shortly after that leaving Vicky with a sense of foreboding and a certainty that for the first time in her marriage, something different had happened in the mind of her husband. She was a little angry that he had rung her in such a state of inebriation. Not that she didn't enjoy a drink from time to time— well they both did, quite regularly. But it was (except for parties and official functions) modest and convivial. Alexei, on the other hand, had obviously had a lot more than normal. The second time in only a few days.

Feeling irritated and concerned she had gone back into the kitchen and met Maria's politely enquiring stare with almost callous indifference. She opened the door to the fridge and removed a bottle of white wine which she had started the evening before. She poured herself a large glass of the stuff and went back into the sitting room. She selected one of her favourite CDs, and its soothing melody, so reminiscent of a long-ago home, filled the room. But it did not ease her state of mind. She could not sit still. Soon she was pacing up and down, taking great gulps of liquid until she found it necessary to go back into the kitchen for a refill, and then, later, change to the thick dark coffee liqueur she was partial to, and which she proceeded to have too much of.

So now, the next morning, her head still heavy with the light fumes of wine and the heavy sweetness of her liqueur, she suddenly found herself completely unfocussed, wondering what on earth her own radio phone-in for the expatriate community was all about.

"I'm sorry," she said again. "What did you say?"

"Hell, Vicky…" (all her regulars called her by her first name even though she had never met most of them). "What's got into you today? I mean I was saying that sure it's wrong to look for love else-where, outside your marriage, but, well, sometimes you just can't help it. You just can't help yourself. Know what I mean?"

"Don't you think…" Her voice faltered as a terrible, earth-shifting thought erupted from somewhere deep inside of her. "… That's a bit too easy? I mean you can always 'help it' can't you? If you want to. Anything else is just a poor excuse to make you feel better. So no, I suppose I don't really know what you mean." She cut him off quickly before she said something she might regret. After all, her programme prospered in its modest way because of her pragmatic evenness.

She went to another caller, an older woman whose voice she recognised immediately because they lived close to each other, and the hour ticked away normally to its end. Somehow she got through it. Somehow, after her momentary lapse, she kept most of her own thoughts in the background and was carried through to the finish by her own acquired professionalism. But when the green light went off and she removed the headphones from her sore ears, there was no escape and she had to face what it was she had suddenly realised about why her husband was acting so strangely.

Jacinto

Half out of carelessness, half out of pride, the great violinist and eminent professor Jacinto Perez left the door of his office slightly open so that students and colleagues rushing backward and forwards along the corridor could hear the magisterial sweetness of his tone as he made his stately progress through the great Chaconne, the undimmed pearl of the solo violinist's repertoire.

Two minutes of preparation while he stood holding his instrument, gradually placing it under his chin, almost fingering the strings with his left hand while the bow hung from his extended right arm, picking up the gathering anticipation of muscle and tendon in their preparatory stirrings, and then seventeen minutes of concentrated amazement as he seemed to become fused with the melodies that he appeared to sing rather than play, and a minute or two of catholic afterglow while the departing music hung like a jewel in the silence of his office. Then the noises from the corridor insinuated themselves past the half-open door and pushed the maestro's magic reluctantly out through the window leaving him nothing but one more memory and the comfortable sensation of pleasure. Now if he could just keep the magic around him like a glittering shield, nothing else would or could intrude and all those awkwardnesses—the sheer horribleness that lurked just outside the door where his life was—could be ignored.

He placed his violin gently back in the open case. With his cloth, he wiped the dusting of powdery rosin from the stick of the bow before loosening the tensed hairs and hooking it into the restraints on the case's lid. All the time he was trying to keep his mind empty, clinging on to the swirl of melody he had so recently released. He knew he was doing it. But when someone knocked on the other side of the door the world was instantly and suddenly with him, pressing its vengeful weight upon his skull.

"Come in," he called reluctantly. The door was pushed open as the student Julio Delgadillo Aceves came into the room, his violin case slung over his back. In his right hand he clasped folders of music. He almost quivered with life. Jacinto was really rather fond of him, quite apart from his obvious talent with his instrument. He was one of the two best students he had at the moment—that is unless one of them was no longer his student. He pushed the thought away. He would deal with it later.

"Ah, Julio," he greeted him, as affably as his present troubles would allow, which was significantly more affable than Julio would normally have expected, "I'm glad you've come."

"Well sir, you left a message in my pigeonhole asking to see me." The boy sounded a little more formal than usual, he thought.

"Well yes, I did. I did. Listen young man, how would you like to be one of the soloists in a concert I'm organising?"

"I don't know. I mean, sir, I'd like it a lot I should think—depending on the piece that is. I mean, of course that would be wonderful sir, I should think." He blushed and ground to a halt, thinking that he had reacted ungratefully. It was always an honour to be a soloist at one of the school's concerts. Sometimes they even got quite good audiences—and not all the people who came were friends and relations.

"Well, as to the piece, I was thinking of the double concerto."

"Oh yes. I mean good. That's good." He had been working on it under the professor's direction for the last few days.

A thought occurred to him. "Who would the other violin be?"

"Yes, well as to that, I thought I might also play."

"You. Sir, did you say you? Sir?"

"Well don't sound too excited about it!"

"No sir. I am. Of course I am. It would be a great honour to play with you, sir. It's not that. It's just that, well, forgive me, you don't usually play in our concerts." Actually, he hardly ever came. The last time he'd attended anything was three weeks ago when he'd listened to Angelita play a sonata in a chamber concert.

Angelita! What would Julio say to her now? Perhaps agreeing to play with the great Jacinto Perez would seem like a betrayal to her. And come to think of it, he didn't much care for the idea of this old man doing that with his friend. To be frank, it disgusted him and when he had asked her to explain how on earth she had got involved in such an inappropriate coupling—though he had put it considerably more gently than that—she had not really been able to explain and had cried a little.

"I'm not talking about one of your concerts," the professor said a little impatiently as if Julio should have known about this, "I'm talking about the opening gala concert of the festival at San Miguel."

"San Miguel? That's where…"

"Yes, I know Julio. That's one of the reasons I thought of you."

"The opening gala concert! Sir, that's fantastic. I mean that's really incredible. But sir, correct me if I'm wrong, but I didn't think you were involved in that opening concert. The posters…"

Jacinto explained about the cancellation and about how he was stepping in with the state orchestra. He would conduct an opening overture, lead the double concerto as one of the two soloists, and then after the interval the orchestra would play the great 'Symphony of a Hundred Moments' by the nation's most famous composer, Arnulfo Villabravo, whose posthumous fame was growing all the time. Such a programme, he thought, mixed gentleness and dignity with power and fury. In its own metaphorical way, it mirrored what it was the Migueleños wished to celebrate.

When Julio left a few minutes later, excited but already a little ashamed by his collusion with the lecherous seducer of his friend, Jacinto was once again left to his own thoughts. He was pleased with his choice of the young violinist. It would enhance the prestige of the National Music School, and surely the people of San Miguel would warm to the sight of one of their own taking a solo spot in such a way, mixing youth with experience. He was sure the boy was up to it both technically and emotionally. He had a natural grace with the instrument and an untroubled confidence that was a pleasure to experience. It should go well.

But it wasn't the concert that mattered. It was that other bit of information Marisol had given him. From the moment the Sons of Perpetual Light had been mentioned Jacinto realised that this was an opportunity he was unlikely to get again. He felt, deeply, that this time something might be achieved. How would it be, he reasoned, if instead of just coming home after a successful concert, he were to walk through the door with the two boys beside him? Every time he thought of it his heart gave a lurch of excitement. There is no joy in Heaven, or, surely, in the Perez household, greater than the prodigals' return. But it was even more than that. Getting the twins back had come to seem, for him, his one great chance for redemption.

Redemption! But who could pronounce him cleansed? His wife, his redoubtable companion, the uncomfortable embodiment of his own conscience? Her absolutions would only be given, he knew, if he once laid before her the complete catalogue of his life's excesses thus far. And he knew that in her eyes, and hearing himself explain with her ears, there was no way in which he could justify himself, no form of words to make the narrative sweet or comprehensible. Her judgement would condemn him utterly.

But how could he be redeemed anyway when his mind was a confused mass of sickly revulsion and obsessive memory? The catastrophe of his seduction of Angelita would not go away. It kept growing, filling the darkness in his mind. It filled his mouth with bile and made him seem to hate the young student who had so defiled him. But the memory of her luminous beauty threatened to fill his every waking thought with longing. He dreamed about her both asleep and awake. He was caught in a vice of shame and sweet nostalgia. Perhaps she could redeem him! But he was not so far gone that he did not realise how ridiculous such a notion really was.

Who then? God? But he had given up belief, partly in response to the disappearance of his sons into some parody of sacred observance, and partly because he had already found his own pleasure and the power of his own creative talent more religiously convincing.

Nevertheless, his upbringing, the Catholic patina over a nation's old gods and images, had taught him about sin and forgiveness so that he knew the power of the one good deed in an otherwise messy life. The retrieval of his sons would be such a deed. It would suffice. Perhaps it could even *borar el pasado*, rub out the past, wash him clean.

Happier now, he turned back to his violin, the altar, and the vestments of the real deity in his life. What will come to pass will come to pass. We can but dream of possibility he told himself. He lifted the instrument from its case again, and tightening the bow, prepared to play.

If not absolution, at least there was escape.

Maria

"Señora," Maria pleaded, "you are very kind and I will always be grateful, for you have saved me when I turned to you for help…"

"Nonsense."

"But you do not have to come up to my apartment with me. I will be all right, I assure you." She was feeling more and more embarrassed and could not bear the thought of further humiliation.

"After everything that has happened," her employer countered imperiously, "I'm afraid I'm going to have to disagree with you, Maria. You need someone to look after you. You will need someone to stop you being taken advantage of. And since there doesn't seem to be anyone else around, why it looks like that someone is me." In truth, Vicky wasn't enjoying this any more than her maid was.

For a moment the injured woman hesitated, pausing on the cracked sidewalk, her hand still resting on the handle of the car door. Even though she knew that Señora Vicky would insist upon it, she still wished there was something she could do to stop her from coming any further. There was no precedent for this, no etiquette for receiving such a person into her home. It made her nervous.

"Señora," she whispered, her voice vanishing into the smoggy air the moment the words were uttered. "Señora, you are kind to bring me here, generous with the offers you make and the help you have given me. But it is that I do not wish to put you to further trouble, señora. I feel already too much in your debt." She knew this to be true. Ever since she had made her way to her employer's door and been comforted and advised by her she had been bound to Vicky more closely than ever before. How will I ever get out of this? she asked herself. What do I do now? What should I say to my—she choked on the thought—my husband?

Maria had not thought very far into the future. She knew that right now she wanted to be as far away from Juan and his unendurable behaviour as she could be. She was relieved to be free of the threat of his violence. Her absence would teach him a lesson. It would be a long absence, she knew that.

Perhaps, then, when it was over, they could go back to a younger, happier marriage, without the cruelty or pain. After all, she had been happy then when they were younger and they had the adventure of the new city to overcome. Now, with no children and little to keep them together except the memory of trouble and past debts, there seemed to be little point to them at all, unless, that is, he was prepared to do something about it. It was up to him. Mend your ways, she would have to say to him, prove to me that you are different. Let me see you lose your temper once and then hold back your hand. Let me see that twice, three times, every time, and then I may even believe you. Except that she probably never would. What a mess. So for now, while she waited to understand what the future was like, she should be allowed to enjoy this sense of freedom, her fear falling off her as the bruises faded back into her soft skin.

For the first few days, buoyed up by the support which Victoria Kassoliniki had given her, Maria lived in a state of hallucinatory exhilaration and confusion. The routine jobs she did in the house seemed somehow sacred. The tiny room they cleared out so that she could sleep there was secure and felt luxurious. Even the children seemed to know that something extraordinary had taken place. But now, in the last couple of days, as her pulse returned to normal and the visions faded, she realised that she was back at her usual job, routine and increasingly pointless, just as before. Her relationship with her employer had lapsed back into an awkward formality, a distant intimacy that they both (Maria was sure) had no idea how to exit from, or maybe develop.

"If you are to live here permanently," Señora Vicky had said, "which is the best solution because I should like it, the children would like it and señor Alex would like it too, wouldn't you like to get some of your things, make your room more homely?"

Of course the answer was *yes*. She wanted the formal photograph of her parents on their wedding day. She longed for the crucifix she had been given for her first communion all those years ago. She needed her underwear and the mirror she combed her hair in front of when she applied the lipstick which she thought made her look more sophisticated.

But she needed Señora Vicky's permission too, and now, she finally admitted to herself, she needed her to help her find the courage to face whatever awaited her when she opened the door of the flat.

She walked across the fractured concrete of the courtyard, the foreign woman at her side as they made their way towards the staircase in the corner. It led to the uneven walkway off which their flat was situated. She knew they were being watched. She cringed at the prospect of what the watchers might be thinking. She lowered her head. Every step seemed to be harder and harder to take.

Señora Vicky took her arm. "Come on," she said, like a parent. "The sooner we start, the sooner it will be over." Upon her insistence, they quickened their stride. Maria looked straight ahead because she thought that if, like a tightrope walker, she looked down or glanced too much to the side, she would lose her balance and perish. In this way, they reached the stairs.

As they started to climb, Maria sensed her companion's distaste at the odours which assailed them. The walls of the stairwell had cracked plaster and everything was covered with a patina of city dirt. She wondered who they might meet. Her breath came in gasps of nervousness at the possibility of it. But they reached the top without incident. The two women stood before the door.

"Well," Vicky said, "aren't you going to open it?" And, for a moment, Maria toyed with the idea of saying she'd lost her key or left it behind by mistake But the moment didn't last. She pulled on the chain to get the ring from her apron pocket. Fitting the right key into the lock, she pushed back the glass and metal door. The scrape as it shaved the stone floor punished her with its familiarity.

Maria and Juan's flat had two rooms: a kitchen and a bed-sitting room with furniture parked upon the floor as if in transit. There was a polythene-covered couch, a plastic table, and three chairs, and an old-fashioned television with a cable leading up to an internal aerial. On the walls were a mirror on a rope string that hung from a nail, a picture of a suffering saint, his red heart exposed so that it generated shafts of celestial light, and a modest crucifix. There was a carefully framed photograph of Maria and her husband standing in one of the capital's parks with its boating lake in the background. It was bleached of colour. Next to the bed on a dark old chest (with its drawers strewn drunkenly open) was an older photo of a couple in wedding clothes holding themselves straight. Apart from that, there was nothing on the walls. The rugs on the floor were frayed, and for Maria (seeing them for the first time through her visitor's eyes), faded and ugly.

On the glass table in front of the couch, an ashtray overflowing with cigarette butts, and four crushed beer cans perched in insolent disorganisation. A disagreeable aroma in the apartment could be traced to the pile of food-encrusted plates in the sink and the over-flowing rubbish which spilled out of its plastic bin. The bed behind them was unmade, a crumpled pair of a man's shorts hanging off the side, the pillows pitted and displaced. Maria's home was a squalid mess.

"Well," Vicky said after they had both stood there in awed silence contemplating the room, "looks like this place has missed a woman's touch these last few days, wouldn't you say?"

"Oh, señora," the woman replied, tears coming to her eyes, her cheeks deep coloured with shame. "Señora, I am mortified. Señora Bicky, it is not right that I have brought you here. I beg your pardon. What must you think? Forgive me."

"Maria, Maria," a hand, astoundingly, again around her shoulder. "It's not your fault. I know you would not let your place get like this. These men! They just can't do without us, can they? They don't deserve us." A darkness flittered briefly across the foreigner's eyes. "Especially not in your case. That's why we're here. So come on, get your things, and let's go."

"But Señora, I can't leave the place looking like this."

"Yes you can. You must. Come on now. Quickly. Before it's too late."

It was when she was loading her few clothes hastily into the string bag she normally used for shopping that she heard someone else come off the walkway into the flat, and knew instantly, without having to turn round, who it must be. Her neighbour Esmeralda had come into the room.

"Maria," she screeched. "My neighbour. Where have you vanished to? Your poor husband, he is beside himself with worry. He is not so good at looking after himself, I think, at looking after anything, it seems." She was studying the mess in Maria's normally tidy apartment and was clearly amazed by what she saw. "What has become of you?" she asked, as if sympathetically. "Where have you been? Maria *de todas las mujeres la mas beneficiada*, have you found a lover?"

She would have replied to that, but she heard Victoria say, "No, of course she hasn't. Mind you, there's no reason why she should not have."

"And, you would be…? Oh no, don't tell me. You're the *gringa*."

"Esmeralda, for the love of God," Maria said.

"Maria's employer, yes, that's who you are," Esmerelda continued, not listening to Maria. "The one she has talked about. The one with the spoilt children and the big house near the park where the rich people live. Foreigners."

"Esmeralda, if you love me, please, enough, stop," Maria implored. Tears trickled down her cheeks now as this terrible day collapsed around her. "Señora," she started to say. "I never..." but she could not go on.

"*¡Ay Maria! mi amiga favorita*, my best friend. I have no wish to cause you any discomfort but I worry for you and for Don Juan, your husband, who has been deserted by his wife."

"So you feel sorry for her husband, do you?" Victoria said.

"Señora," Maria wailed. "Please, I beg you..."

"Yes, of course I feel sorry for him. Abandoned by his wife.

Though she is my friend, this Maria, that is the only word I can use. Abandoned, deserted, as no husband should be, left alone…"

Maria heard her voice droning on, the moralising blur of it that she had come to know so well. She had tried to train herself to ignore most of it. You make of neighbours what you can. They are on the same team. Esmeralda was her friend, of a kind.

"Look," she heard her employer cut in, "we're in a bit of a hurry, so I wonder, perhaps, if you could stop giving Maria such a hard time. And by the way, that husband of hers, *deserted*, I think you said, or was it abandoned? What kind of a husband is it that beats his wife?"

"*¡Ay Maria!*" Esmeralda protested, ignoring Vicky completely, her face grotesque in surprise. It was as if she had never heard the shouting or the tears or the collisions with the furniture. "You have been beaten? Well, that is news to me. But of course you would probably have been beaten, even though I have not known of it. You are a woman. All wives are beaten sometimes. What does this *gringa* know of it?"

"This *gringa*, as you call her," Victoria continued, "knows plenty, especially that no one, do you hear me, no woman, in this block of apartments, in this city, in this country, in the whole damn world, no woman has to put up with abuse from a man whether it's husband, father, brother or lover. Which is why 'neighbour' or whoever you are, Maria is not staying here but is coming with me instead."

"*Sí,* to San Miguel where I will be even safer," Maria said happily, before meeting her employer's appalled gaze. Surely there was no harm in mentioning it. When Señora Bicky had announced that she had to go to San Miguel de las Colinas and that the children would have to go with her, and that meant Maria, too—if it was all right with her—the maid had said *yes, of course, why not?* Her employer had spoken quickly and urgently as if the trip were vitally important. Now, in the flat, her next words, therefore, came as something of a surprise.

"To San Miguel? Perhaps not. We might go somewhere else entirely."

"*Si señora patrona.* Somewhere else." Esmeralda had a nasty glint in her censorious eye.

Unable to comprehend exactly what was happening in this conversation she nevertheless managed to propel her neighbour, who was now returning to the theme of wifely desertion, out onto the walkway. Then she took her things and, with her employer's encouragement, closed the door behind them both as they left to make their way back down the stairs and across the courtyard to the waiting car. She could not believe she had left the place looking such a mess. Clutching her crucifix as Señora Bicky pulled out behind two old buses, she knew with a sudden, almost physical lurch, that things would never be the same again.

Angelita

SHE ALWAYS HATED the beginnings and endings of bus journeys. She hated the moment when she found herself cramped in the small aisle between the seats, behind people who always seemed to take far too long to move forward. It was almost as bad as being on an aeroplane, though her impecunity as a student, despite her father's mild generosity, meant she rarely travelled that way. But this morning, much earlier than she would have wanted to be awake, as she struggled down the aisle to find her seat, her large bag bouncing off the seats on her right, her leather bag threatening to slip off her shoulder, she found the claustrophobic interior of the bus more difficult to bear than usual. She was sweating and the city's noxious exhalations clung to her like dirt.

She did not want to be travelling. She wanted only the silence of her room and the chance to continue reassessing her life. She wanted to talk to Julio some more. He was a kind and understanding friend. But she had no option but to be here now. She had not been able to reach him to say she was leaving.

When Tia Rosario had rung to give them the news, her father had been almost relieved to have something to talk to his daughter free from the awkwardness that had developed ever since she had come home that day looking, to his eyes, anxious and upset. Of course, Federico didn't want his father to get sick, least of all to have his ultimate survival threatened. Nor, you could be sure, did he know what it would be like to face the world alone. He still felt, as far as Angelita could tell, the need to prove himself even after all this time.

"A heart attack," Tia Rosario had said, Federico told his daughter, "or something very like it. They're not quite sure. But he is not looking very well if I speak the truth, and if God wants to take him, he may do it soon." Federico had put down the phone confused, panic mixed with an unavoidable irritation at this interruption. What should he do? The cement worker case was just at this moment becoming critical; he couldn't leave it. Yet here was his father again, demanding attention and obedience. That's what it felt like in those first few minutes as he digested Tia Rosario's news. When Angelita came in, pale and listless as she had been for the last few days he said to her, "What should I do? Run to San Miguel? And lose this case because I'm not there when the judge wants me? So I betray the workers who have put their trust in me? And then your grandfather is not so ill after all, and I have messed up everything? Is that what I should do?"

"I don't know Papa. What do you think you should do?"

"*¡Ay, mi hija!* I am so unsure. He can not be so ill, surely. Not your grandfather. Not him. My aunt is exaggerating. She must be. God, what am I going to do?"

She looked at him, saw the crease lines across his forehead, the skin drained of all its elasticity by perplexity and nicotine, the white pinpricks of stubble upon his jaw, and thought, as if for the first time, that he looked older. This did not help her to advise him. She was suddenly overcome with a surge of love for him. She hugged him, kissed him on the cheek, and ruffled his hair as only his daughter would be permitted to do.

"Tell you what," she said as the thought occurred to her. "Why don't I go up and see if Tia Rosario is being overly dramatic or what. I'll go and see *mi abuelo*, my grandfather, and then if things are serious I'll call you and you can fly up."

It made her feel good, this assumption of responsibility. Her father frequently denied her the chance for such displays. He merely said, "What about your studies?" She wondered how he could have failed to notice that she had hardly been studying or practising at all recently. Her violin had remained obstinately in its case, pushed unceremoniously beneath the bed.

Even her routine had changed. She went in to meet Julio and some other friends at lunchtime. She hung around that part of the city in the afternoons and sometimes went out in the evenings if Julio had nothing to do. But the regular timetable of lessons and lectures and practice and performance had been abandoned ever since she had been so rudely awakened from the addictive sleep of passion. Any moment now, she'd be thrown out of the school, but she did not know how to go back there.

The figure of her teacher had grown oversized and shaming in her imagination. She did not think she had the courage to encounter him and still stay upright. Yet her father, despite being worried by her general appearance, had not realised how much her life had changed, bound up as he was in a battle for justice which this time he might just win. So when he asked the question she just said, "There's no problem with my studies. I can get time off," and he didn't question it.

Here she was, reaching up to put her bag on the rack above row 17 at an uncomfortable hour of the morning, feeling important and frustrated, but slightly relieved, despite everything, at her escape. She eased herself into the seat. She nodded a greeting to the middle-aged woman in the seat next to the window, and took a magazine and a book from her bag in case she was not able to sleep. Through the window beyond her neighbour, she could see the driver throwing cases into compartments underneath them. A bus pulled into the bay beside them. She heard the roar of its engine suddenly contained and the smack of its opening door.

She watched the passengers disembarking, bleary-eyed in the city dawn. She wondered what emergencies they were all heading towards, whether they came in fear or hope. She thought again of her beloved grandfather, old and idiosyncratic, who loved her. She closed her eyes and conjured up pictures of him teasing her, his eyes alight; pictures of him watching her intently then taking her girlish hand in his vast paw with its rough pads and fleshy fingers. She dreamed herself into the magic comfort of the house in San Miguel and for the first time since her father told her the news, she suddenly felt sad and afraid, as if she really might lose the old man to whom nothing ever had to be explained.

Lost in her reverie, her eyes closed, she sensed the last few passengers get on, heard the door hiss shut, and felt the large vehicle back out of its bay, engine revving discordantly until with a lurch of forward movement they were off. She could work out when they left the bus depot and when they turned right onto the inner circle, the stop-start-stop of city traffic, even at this time of the morning.

With a resigned determination she forced her eyes to stay shut despite the light which threatened to spring them open. Her book and magazine were held firmly on her lap. She even began to think she really might sleep as they approached the toll at the entrance to the main autoroute. She was aware that they slowed down to pass between the collection booths before the acceleration lurched out from the engine behind them and they were off in the sharp tang of the morning, diesel fumes pumping black into the warming air, the motor roaring up and down the scale to satisfy the driver's increasing desire for speed.

It was comfortable now that they were travelling at a steady pace. She absorbed the rhythms of the wheels, allegro ma non troppo, steady beating, and for once the engine noise seemed more like a lullaby than a threat. She was drifting away into more dreams of her grandfather's fond smile and the unquestioning welcome that would await her, even from her great-aunt. She thought of Marcelita's grin of unconscious happiness, the old man's welcoming arms. She was overcome with nostalgia and a sudden what-would-I-do-if-he-was-no- longer-there? which warmed her even as it made her fearful. She hugged her arms around her for foetal comfort.

Except that at that very moment, it would not work. Something from her left had crept in on her, invading her consciousness. She shifted her weight, feeling the magazine and book lurch for a brief moment before she re-established her equilibrium. She screwed her eyelids deeper into each other hoping that the darkness within would prove an effective barrier against whatever alien presence was making itself known to her. The bus leaned into a sharp motorway bend so that Angelita, who had travelled this route so many times before, knew exactly where they were, and could picture the countryside on either side of the road, the dirty home-made shacks of the city-headed families on one side with their makeshift electricity and inadequate sewage disposal, and the plain gradually rising up to the mountains on the other, cousins to the gnarled old volcanoes they had left behind them.

The knowledge of where they were, and the picture this knowledge played past her retina were enough to destroy any further hope of sleep. However hard her eyes were closed, they were, like her thoughts and idiosyncratic perceptions, active and alert. Turning her head away from the source of her discomfort so that she lay sideways against the headrest, she opened her eyes. The woman beside her was fast asleep, she noted enviously. Her head had fallen forward towards her chest, her bottom lip loosely opened in sleep. Angelita could hear the rhythm of her breath clashing with the steady beat of their journey. She turned her face away, her eyes revolving over the aisle until with the shock of collision they met the gaze of the man sitting across from her, a tall foreign-looking person, a few years her senior, who was staring at her with a haunted intensity that bruised her senses.

"Ah, you're awake," he said in an accented voice. "You're the musician."

She thought of closing her eyes again so that she could escape his direct stare, but his attention held her so that now she was really awake.

"I'm sorry," she said. "What was that?" You could ignore most men and their attempts to make contact but it was more difficult when they were sitting less than a metre away and there was no way of getting rid of them.

"You're the musician—a violinist I thought. I don't really know what you play. I saw you on the metro recently. In the afternoon. Early evening. You looked sad, troubled. I wondered why. I thought you were beautiful."

He stopped dead in his tracks and went bright red.

Angelita turned away, staring intently into the seat back in front of her. She supposed she might, vaguely, remember him, the strange eyes puncturing, for a moment, her own orgy of upset and confusion on that day. Madre, yes, that day. She'd wanted it to fade away. Some hope. Well, at least she'd got her period a few days ago so one part of the nightmare, at least, was past. But sin like that sticks to you, she supposed and you can't wipe it clean, not even sealed up in a bus on the way to visit your sick grandfather.

"You haven't got your instrument with you," the foreigner said, breaking into her thoughts as if he was her friend. She liked his voice, resonant but uncertain, his strange pronunciation unsettling her. He wasn't a typical gringo, it appeared. She found it suddenly difficult to be as angry with him as she wanted to be.

"No," she replied, "I haven't." She turned and looked at him. He was fair-skinned with traces of sun masking his city pallor. His eyes, she noticed, were light blue, almost colourless in the bus light, and the mouth beneath the prominent nose finished in an uneven smile. The line between his eyebrows was etched deep with unease.

"Forgive me," he said, holding his hand out across the aisle as if this absurd bus were some kind of social arena, "I do not mean to trouble you. I do not usually—that is, you have nothing to fear from me. My name is Martin."

To her surprise, Angelita found herself offering her own hand in return. More extraordinarily, she realised that she was smiling.

"Hello, Martin," she said and felt, for the first time, the touch of his fingers upon her.

Marisa

THOUGH SHE LIVED in a world of perpetual dreams, only overseeing the rituals of daily life with a casual automaticity, learned in years of quotidian repetition, Marisa Sepulveda de Perez nevertheless knew that something was wrong with her son. More than this, she knew her husband was involved or was even the cause of it. Her husband! The man who all those years ago she had allowed to fill her with dreams of ecstasy made flesh, persuading her fleetingly that physical pleasure was somehow more pressing than the world of spirits she owed her first allegiance to. What foolishness. For when it was no longer possible to achieve the climaxes of pleasure which had so overwhelmed her, what would be left if the spirits her mother had taught her to listen to had departed long ago in protest at her treatment of them?

For as long as her daughter could remember, Marisa's mother had worked as a cleaner at a hotel right in the middle of the city. Once the building had been peaceful and elegant, but then, as the fumes enveloped it and traffic intensified the vibrations in its old stones, it lapsed into squalid mediocrity. Its clientele changed as if the day had changed into the night, so that instead of week-long habitations people booked rooms by the afternoon, even, at a pinch, by the hour, and still the chambermaids, lead by the redoubtable old hawk, Marisa's mother, would pull used sheets off beds, clear away the detritus of another occupation, and puff up the pillows in preparation for new businessmen, truckers or tarts.

Once Marisa had made it big in the world of music and then, by marrying the violinist, had ended up rich, she tried to persuade her mother to stop working in such a humiliating milieu. But her mother was grounded in her job. Though she had complained about it, she had liked what she did because she was used to it, and knew the ins and outs of it, its limits, and its boundaries. It was something she did, quite distinct from the world that her one child, the opera singer, had inherited.

Marisa's mother had liked to claim that she came from the old world, harking back to the exploits of her ancestor and his descendants in defence of the old power which brought a religion from across the sea to tame them all. Except, of course, that the old woman had always demanded the right to stray outside that belief into earlier mythology, where, she told people, the dead spoke to her. She said that she believed herself to be a channel for their nostalgia and for their desperate attempts to organise the world along the lines that their ethereal presences thought desirable.

From early childhood, therefore, Marisa could remember the neighbours who came round for consultations with the army of those who rejoiced upon another shore, separated from this world by the extra-present dimension they inhabited. Marisa's mother had put widows in touch with their departed husbands, enabled mothers to talk to their still-born children, and had spoken, through her rasping larynx, the vowels of long-dead lovers, the consonants of loss and hope.

It had taken the opera singer all the years of her childhood and adolescence to persuade her mother to tell her how she had been conceived, to tease out from her the shameful admission that, given the time in question, she could quite well have been the progeny of either of two or possibly three lovers from the time after the rains the year before the year of her birth. When she remonstrated with her mother about this, the older woman fixed glistening eyes upon her, grasped her hand in her thin fist, and said but why should you complain? I have given you two and a half fathers. What child could

142

be more fortunate? That was long after they had discovered the gift of Marisa's extraordinary voice, long after she had established herself as a star.

When she considered the three potential seed-givers she failed to find any point of contact with any of them. Though like any rational being, she disbelieved the reality of immaculate conception, still she thought the fact of her own creation was more magical than messy. Despite the fact that her intellect, which could have been considerable, related to her the facts of her mother's multiple insem-inations, her heart told her a story of a life made by the harmony of an ethereal choir. The image of the spirits her mother talked to peopled her childhood loneliness and against all the precepts of her reason, they still informed her every action, taking her back into a silent world that filled her head with voices.

When Marisa was a child, unfathered yet oppressed by all the dead people her mother was a channel for, she had started to dream, and soon her every night was a cacophony of voices; gods she had heard of in school, personages drawn from scraps and moanings in the home where the seances took place. They were quite real to her. She could see their faces, hear their voices, and know how they were dressed. They were like characters from a storybook that had been left unillustrated and whose empty pages, therefore, she was obliged to draw on. Down the years they never changed or aged, though some disappeared and other characters forced themselves upon her.

Sometimes she could swear they were more real than the people on the streets around her. These were ideal spirits built with the bricks of her own girlish longing. They became so present in her life that she let them talk to her whenever she was alone, whether waking or sleeping. When adversity struck—when friends were cruel or her mother unloving—it was to the cast in her head that she went for comfort rather than to any acquaintance of real flesh and blood. After one disastrous humiliation when she told a school friend about her world and was hurtfully mocked, her other-worldly spirits stayed locked inside her. Later she knew, with absolute certainty, to keep them secret from the man who fathered children upon her.

Once, when the music was strong in her and her voice had

moved thousands, Marisa had allowed herself to abandon the figures from her past, the multitudes who gathered round her when she was alone. They had retreated beyond the reach of her dreams and daytime reveries. The songs had been too present, the melodies too sweeping to allow their voices space to penetrate. And then, just when it seemed that they might be able to make their way back into her mind the violinist had appeared with his commanding presence and the promise of earthly delight. Instead of which he had filled her with seed so that she, in her turn, had produced new life to distract her and claim her attention. Then the twins drowned out the music and the spirits came back to keep her company. Her secret existence, temporarily suppressed, re-surfaced calling back a life she had thought abandoned all those years ago.

She started to dream again, welcoming back her characters like old friends, listening to them while she changed nappies or held first one and then the other twin to her breasts, talking to her boys when she thought no one else was listening, and finally introducing them to her ethereal friends. They all seemed to get on well together and the boys, almost as soon as they could think, realised that this world should remain secret from their father. They did not know that he had his own demons to confront. They just knew that he was different and definitely not part of their world. Even when he was at home—which was less than children might reasonably expect from a father—he seemed strange, an outsider, excluded from the tight knot of mother and sons and all the others he knew nothing about.

Then the boys were gone. Yet how could Jacinto know that Marisa was sure it was all her fault that they had turned away from the world of their parents? She understood that they had been forced to find an escape from the spirit world she had immersed them in and was convinced that their embrace into a new family was a rejection of her continual peculiarity. She told her spirits that they had betrayed her.

She tried to show them what damage they had wrought, and once again presumed to abandon them. But she could not. They were too used to her attempts to banish them. They always found a way back. Whether she sat at the dinner table or rode a taxi through the streets after yet another of her uninteresting husband's interminable concerts or a music school prize-giving, she was conscious of their voices and could not stop hearing their comments. You don't want to do that, they would tell her, perhaps you weren't such a good singer anyway. We're the only reason you're around. And now, after all these years, she could no longer pretend that they were not real. It was far too late for that.

When she had tried to tell her mother about her familiars—long before they had taken such a hold upon her—the old woman had rebuffed her in a tirade of typical acerbity. "Spirits?" she'd snorted. "What nonsense is this, Marisa?"

"But you talk with the dead, mother."

"Well, yes. Be that as it may. My people need to be comforted. That's the main thing. Don't you think?" It was an answer that helped to obscure the true meaning of the seances as completely as ever.

After sex and birth, it was only food that silenced her voices, since the act of eating engaged parts of her brain normally reserved for the functioning of other senses. When she needed time to think, without their interruption, she ate more and more, consuming with a passion so that her body's natural proclivity for adipose deposits soon teetered close to clinical obesity, and her stare, as a result, was a searchlight of baleful disapproval.

It is possible that Marisa had become somewhat mad, yet she was sane enough not to let the spirits interfere with her third son, convinced as she was that they had ruined the first two. She told him nothing of them and was consequently silent a lot of the time for reasons that the young boy could not fathom but which, coupled with his father's evasions, soon began to look like an absence of love. He concluded, over the years, that the strange distance between his two parents was the result of his own inadequacy. He wasn't good at anything. Puberty only exaggerated his discomfort since it gave him unsatisfied longings and an erupting face.

Unlovely and insecure, he retreated to his own kingdom of alienation thinking himself protected from failure there, but still relying, at least, on the external certainties of his miserable world, a mother, a father, a sense of cold order. But then, the sight of his father doing that with a girl not that much older than himself ruptured the thin membrane which kept him sane. It was so shocking that he was completely unnerved. He had absolutely no idea what to do or how to survive the chaos in his head.

"What is it, my love?" his mother said sometime later when Jacinto had left for the music school, from where he would fly to San Miguel later in the day to start preparing for the big concert. The poor boy was so surprised at her sudden concern that his confusion only increased. But she patted him, taking care not to come into contact with his face or the greasy hair which clothed it, and fretted.

Francisco had to think of something to say to stop himself from blurting out the big thing that he had seen. That was unsayable. But his suggestion, when he thought of it, that they should follow his professor-father to San Miguel, was not. Something about it seemed right. It seemed to please his mother too since she agreed immediately.

Mother and unbalanced son climbed into the big car together, to start the long drive north.

Martin

HE FELT comfortable sitting beside her, light-hearted, as if everything was all right and he had known her for ever. She didn't seem inclined to judge him half as harshly as he usually judged himself. It wasn't like talking to a 'girl' either, even if he hadn't been too old for that, and too damaged. It was just like talking to a real friend who happened to be extraordinarily beautiful. But not in that way, he thought, even if it was what he had noticed first when he'd seen her on the downtown metro that day.

Oh come on, he remonstrated, *you hardly know her.* She probably thinks nothing of you. You can't feel that good after a short time on a bus. He was still reeling from the shock of having dared to speak to her in the way he had done when, at the beginning, he found himself sitting across the aisle from her.

It was the woman sitting next to Angelita who had said, "Here, young man, why don't you change places with me? You and the young woman seem to be getting on so well!"

It was when they had been about to get back on board after they'd been stuck on the side of the motorway. The driver had to replace the accelerator cable, which had snapped at the top of the long incline just past the village of La Princesa.

It was said in all friendliness and, of course, it was true. They were. Already Angelita had told him that she was a music student and that her grandfather, who was ill, lived in San Miguel and she was going to see him and that that was why she was on the bus. She described the old man and talked about her great-aunt and her simple cousin. She enjoyed telling him all this. She did not tell him about a professor old enough to be her father and the touch of his scaly skin on hers. But she thought she knew she would.

Martin, in his turn, talked of how he had come here, and of his sister and her work on the radio. He went on a bit about his niece and nephew whom he loved and tried to describe the bearded vulcanologist who was so much part of his family and explained how, after their fashion, they had even come to respect each other in a way. He did not tell her about shotguns in the mouth or about a girl falling, falling with her eyes open and the knowledge of death upon her. But he thought that he knew that he would.

It wasn't as if the music student had suddenly, at a stroke, kilometre by kilometre, put the harmonies back into the desiccated melody of Martin's life. It would take more than a bus ride to do that. But the ease with which he could talk to her was encouraging. He found himself smiling as he spoke, instead of stretching his forehead in his usual frown, or looking disconsolately at the backs of his hands, something Vicky made fun of him about. Instead, he met her eyes and held her stare without turning away. Instead of looking into the distance in some unfocussed melancholy when they had stood by the roadside in the bright sunshine after the breakdown they had laughed right into each other's eyes. The wind of the high plain and the tear of passing vehicles yanked their hair into fantastic patterns, thrusting her luxurious curls across her face so that she had to keep pushing them away.

All of the passengers, a suddenly cohesive group, seemed in remarkably good spirits, cracking jokes about the driver, the bus company, the motorway, national transport, the government, and all the other old favourites of a cynical people whose hopes for a more innocent existence were constantly eroded by the venality of the people who had bribed and compromised their way into power. The driver—there was only one driver all the way from the capital to

San Miguel—had born their good-humoured moaning with, initially, demonstrations of relaxed laughter.

Half submerged in the rump of the powerful vehicle, he had thrown remarks back over his shoulder to counteract the jokes that flowed around him. But as the minutes passed, turning into half an hour and then three-quarters of an hour while he wrestled with the recalcitrant cables and his crisp blue company shirt acquired patches of oil and grease, his replies were fewer and his levity became less pronounced.

By the time he clicked the metal rod back into position, slammed the engine grill shut, and fastened it with his key, it was clear that he was thoroughly fed up. He barked at them all to re-board, quickly, we've lost a lot of time here (as if it was all their fault). A male passenger said wistfully that he didn't design the *pinche* bus. He wasn't even responsible for its maintenance. The driver pretended he hadn't heard, but instead gunned his engine and roared back onto the motorway with every appearance of bad grace.

They had left the autoroute and started the seventy-kilometre stretch of curves, which Angelita knew so well. One moment, they were hard into a vertical rock face with its dangers of falling stones and ragged lives, the next, they turned sharply right to find the land dropping away suddenly so that any miscalculation could send them plunging over a cliff top to their certain death. In the hands of a good driver and at the right speed, the mocking corners, first this way, then that, were like a lullaby, intimate and insinuating, but driven by someone less sure—or someone hell-bent on driving too fast—they were awkward, spine-shaking and terrifying.

Martin had been listening to Angelita's worries about getting to San Miguel in time. She wanted to make sure her dear *abuelo* was all right. Then, she could ring her father and tell him not to worry and not to jump onto a plane when there was no real urgency. At that moment, the bus lurched over to the left. Through the charcoal tint of the window, they looked down on the old van they were passing, very fast. They heard their coach driver swear, shouting as if someone outside on the road could hear him.

Through the front window ahead of them, they could see a line of oncoming traffic. The bus engine roared to power them past a slower van and then they were bevelling into a corner, shock absorbers squashed right down on one side as if they would never make it. Someone in front of Martin and Angelita screamed.

Martin said, "Fuck me!" and then, realising that his companion might not understand what he was saying, he changed it to "*¡Hijo de puta!* Son of a bitch that was a bit scary!"

Federico's daughter laughed at him and said, "That's just the way we drive here. You're not used to it, that's all." But the sudden pallor of her face hollowed out her words.

It got worse. Each corner seemed to force more combat from the man in front. The howl of the engine as it went through the gear changes and the discordant engagement of the brakes unsettled everyone as the vehicle swayed unevenly. There were mutterings all through the bus now, and occasionally audible gasps and exclamations. Martin caught the old woman looking out of the window as they skirted yet another precipice. She clasped a devotional book upon her lap. She closed her eyes to stop the fear but kept having to open them again to check that things were still OK. Her lips started to move in a whispered prayer for deliverance.

"I may not be used to it," Martin said as lightly as he could, staring straight into Angelita's hazel eyes and realising, through his unease, how sweet they were, "but this guy's got some kind of a death wish or something. He's throwing this bus around as if he wants to kill us all."

She didn't answer for a moment. She was holding on to the metal handle on the seat back in front of her as the bus leaned over to the right and the driver's side wheels almost left the ground. This time a passenger two rows ahead screamed quite loudly. "Slow down!" a woman shouted, but her voice was not strong and the driver's head and shoulders showed no movement to suggest that he had heard.

Angelita grabbed his arm. "Can't someone tell him to go slower?" she said, plaintively. She was frightened now. She looked like the first time he had seen her—a stranger in distress. And she was appealing to him, however ridiculous that seemed. He had no choice.

Bracing himself against the vehicle's erratic movement he staggered down the aisle, hanging on to the seat backs for dear life. When he got to the front he had to summon all his physical strength to place himself on the steps, his back to the door, facing the driver who stared through the large windscreen with a kind of manic intensity.

Everyone was watching him. Angelita's white face willed him on.

"Hey look, sorry to interrupt you, I don't want to distract you or anything, but is there any chance…"

"Get back to your seat," the driver barked, not turning round. Martin noticed his muscled forearms as he pulled them round another curve.

"You're not supposed to be here," the man told his passenger who had nearly lost his footing. "Not safe. Go and sit down."

"OK, OK, I will. I promise. But couldn't you slow down a bit?"

"What? What are you talking about?"

"It's just that everyone's frightened. They think you're driving too fast. I mean I'm sure there's no problem, but just to make everyone feel better couldn't you…"

"*¡Chinga tu madre!* Screw your mother! Are you telling me how to drive, *gringo*?"

"No, of course not. But we don't think it's safe, see, the speed you're going. Slow down. Please. That's all we're asking."

He felt quite angry now, provoked by the man's attitude, frightened by the road so close beyond the glass. Behind him, on that side of the bus, there was a drop of about two hundred feet. They wouldn't stand a chance if they went down that. In front of them, the road curved back round to the left and disappeared behind exposed stone slabs on a precipitous hillside. Here and there the tarmac was pitted with cracks and small holes.

The driver wasn't going to listen to him. He wasn't going to change his behaviour unless Martin could think of something compelling. He found himself staring through the windscreen at an incongruous sight; a battered old taxi from the capital—the only place where taxis were that colour as far as he knew—and they were getting closer all the time. The old car in front was having trouble negotiating the slopes and bends, it seemed.

Martin suddenly remembered something Vicky had told him. Once, when he was travelling, she said, Alexei had been really scared by the driver of the taxi he was in, and he was desperate to get him to slow down. In a flash of inspiration, he had found the perfect threat. That's it, Martin thought, I'll try that. I don't have anything to lose.

"Look," he said, changing the tone of his voice, keeping belligerence right out of it. "My.." he hesitated. "My *compañera*, my companion back there isn't feeling too well."

He leant forward, bending down so that he was level with the man's face. "And I'm really worried she's going to throw up—you know with the speed, the corners. There's a danger she's going to vomit all over your bus."

"She'd better not. Tell her to control herself. Use a plastic bag. Use your head. Now go and sit down and stop talking to me. You're not supposed to get in my way."

The bus surged forward, pulling out into the oncoming lane to pass the struggling taxi. It was a suicidal manoeuvre. There was a blind corner ahead and it was far too close.

My God, Martin thought, *if anything is coming the other way we'll all be dead.*

Something was coming the other way—another inter-city bus came powering round the bend. A collision seemed inevitable.

"You crazy bastard!" he shouted, quite out of character. "You're killing us!"

"Go screw yourself!" the driver replied, pushing the bus even faster and then, just as the two giants were about to smash into one another, head on, he yanked the wheel to the right to get out of the way.

The oncoming vehicle passed within a few centimetres of them, its lights flashing, its horn blaring anger and fear. Martin saw the white faces of the passengers as they narrowly shaved by.

Now the road corkscrewed into another s-bend. At this speed, it seemed impossible that they would avoid catastrophe. It was the rock face or the void for them. But the driver pulled with all his strength, forcing the tires screaming into the hot tarmac, desperate to save himself.

Everyone on the bus would have known that it was not going to work. They all felt the dragon-tail swipe as its back end swatted the old taxi they were passing. They felt the vehicle lift up like a sailboat, and then it was too late because it tipped right over. They were down on one side, screaming along the road in a howling nightmare of breaking glass and lacerated metal, gouging runnels out of the tarmac as they went. When they finally came to a rest, they heard the dreadful one-note of a car horn behind them bleating out into a shocked silence. Then the crying and howling started.

Far above the road, the *zopilotes* hovered optimistically.

Maria

SHE HAD NEVER TRAVELLED on the highway in a car like this. For a start the windows were closed because, Señora Bicky explained, the air-conditioning system was just the latest and worked really well. No noise got into the passenger compartment from outside despite the fact that they were going much faster than she had ever gone in the taxi or the third-class buses she had taken on the rare occasions when she went back to her *tierra*.

She sat between Daniel and Sarah, half of her mind occupied with looking after them, and some of what was left over listening out for what her employer might say. She had to stop thinking about how much she was enjoying herself.

She had been surprised the other day when the Señora had said they were going to San Miguel. It wasn't like her to come up with sudden decisions like that. On the contrary, the rhythm of the house never changed. She knew what time the children's mother went to work. She knew that she worked on the radio and had, on more than one occasion, heard her voice coming out of the speakers, though she had understood nothing of what was said.

Maria was familiar with the time the taxi driver (not Juan, though he had asked her to get him the job) arrived to pick up the children and take them to their school. She knew where the sheets

154

were kept, what kind of underwear her employers used, and how to use the different settings on the expensive steam iron that she secretly coveted. At least it didn't frighten her unlike the new kitchen which had just been installed and which, with its dials and computerised controls, was incomprehensible. The señora had tried to explain the various devices to her on many occasions, but something in her mind would not allow her to understand what was being said. Instead, she reverted to the things she was used to (the metal *plancha* and the gas ring, much to señora Bicky's great amusement).

Sometimes she thought it was wrong that people like them should live like that while she and her husband lived the way they did. When Juan taunted her about it, she was ashamed. Often she thought that the two children of her employers were disrespectful of their parents—and especially of her—but she told herself that since she had not been given the chance to experience motherhood herself, she was not really in a position to judge. All she knew was that her employer seemed a decent enough sort of person. She obviously loved her family, and was herself loved by her husband, a strange almost God-like kind of character, Maria had sometimes thought. The children had both of their parents in them, carrying a mixture of their mother's friendly welcome and their father's strangeness. They were little aliens, Maria thought. They took her breath away even before they ran around her.

Maria had thought that her life would never change: the beatings, the taxi drives through the smog, the vast spaces of the Kassoliniki house, the fear at the end of the day, and her inevitable humiliation.

But now, everything was different. Her employer, normally so controlled and controlling, seemed uncharacteristically disorganised. This morning she had not put on any make-up, Maria noticed, and wisps of hair were escaping from the clip which normally held all of it tightly clasped. In the night, she had woken to hear noises from the kitchen and, her legs shaking with the fear of confronting an intruder, she had crept out of her room and had dared to look in (without being seen), Señora Bicky knocking back the contents of a glass from one of her foreign bottles, puffing away on a cigarette, a habit she had said she'd abandoned a year before.

Maria should have been surprised. Yet ever since a few days ago when, Maria knew, she had talked to the señor, her employer had been like this, uncertain, agitated, and snappy. When she had taken Maria to get her things from her flat something had been wrong—a fact Maria only noticed when looking back at that strange day and her neighbour's horrible words.

What did she really understand about all this? What really mattered was that this woman—this family—was giving her shelter at a time when she needed to get away. If that meant a long car journey, a trip out to a place Maria had never been to and knew nothing about, that was a small price to pay for a skin free from bruises and a few weeks untroubled by her violent companion.

The children were bouncing up and down on either side of her, chattering away in their own language. "Hush," the maid said seeing her mistress' troubled eyes in the rear-view mirror, "your mother needs to concentrate on what she's doing." This was the excuse Juan had always given for not listening to her when they drove. Daniel Kassoliniki was not convinced and started to sing some nonsense rhyme about burros and donkeys. Then he and his sister burst into fits of giggles, and their mother, Maria noticed, watching her eyes, forced a grimace that was not like her usual smile.

Although she was concerned with her own troubles, and ill at ease with the sudden change in her circumstances, Maria had understood enough to know that they were driving to find Señor Alexei. Something important rested on this. Obviously, something wasn't right, and it was clear that Señora Bicky was taking them to San Miguel to sort it out.

She had said something about the Señor not being well and that he needed her. At first, she had pictured him ill in hospital, but the señora had said something about his mountain work which suggested he was still up and about so it couldn't be that. My, but life's a funny thing, me running away from my husband and my employer running towards hers as fast as she could.

They had left the motorway some time ago. Sarah had fallen asleep now, her child's head heavy on Maria's thigh as she dreamed.

The boy Daniel, older, resolutely older, sat staring out of the window, yawning occasionally, keen to keep watch.

Maria was beginning to feel a bit sick as the car twisted this way and that, *"Mil curvas,"* Señora Bicky said, "that's what they call this road Alexei says. You can understand why!"

Now they were descending a long slope, a sheer drop to their left, the steep hillside on their right. The evening sun was on the point of slipping behind the mountains. It was beautiful, golden. Señora Bicky was a fast driver. But she braked as she approached a blind right-hand curve at the bottom.

"Look!" she said, and Maria followed the pointing arm she had taken from the wheel to indicate the tyre scars on the road and the ruptured concrete of the little roadside marker. There were pieces of tin at the road's edge and a diamond dusting of glass fragments. "There must have been a nasty accident here," she said.

As they rounded the corner they saw evidence of an even greater collision: more glass, a twisted hub cap, and black scourings of rubber parallel tracked but then crossed over until they finished abruptly and were replaced by livid white wounds on the road's surface. The hillside was gouged out. There was fresh mud like spilled guts. Bits of metal lined the road. A green tourist truck was parked there, its orange light flashing, its driver and passenger in fluorescent jackets picking pieces up off the roadside.

"There must have been at least two accidents here," Señora Vicky said. "Earlier today, I should think to judge from the mess—I mean they must have taken whatever it was away. I wonder what happened."

"¡Santa Maria llena de gracia!" Maria intoned, "I hope no one died, and if they did, may the Lord take them to live with him in paradise."

The air-conditioned car with its foreign driver, sleeping children (both of them now), and the liberated maidservant coasted past the residue of whatever accident had happened. Safely, it continued its journey toward San Miguel and an attempt to resolve a crisis.

Federico

On the way back home in the metro, Federico Hernandez Placencia tasted the knowledge of his victory sourly. He might have experienced pleasure when, finally, the employers had caved in and the cement workers were reinstated and, what's more, on an increased salary. But then, he had realised that far from being the judgement of a fair-minded member of the judiciary, swayed by his arguments about justice and humanity, the decision was mostly based on a massive bribe that the union had paid to the cement company. That way they combined the pretence of winning battles for their workers with political expediency and the employers were compensated for any embarrassment and any temporary increase in the salary bill.

Was it always to be like this? he pondered as they hummed through the late afternoon. Was his father right after all about the way things were done, had always been done, and would always be done? *¡Fuerza major!* The strongest and the richest always triumph. Never the little people.

Oh God, the arguments they had fought, the campaigns they had waged in their wars of attrition, both of them inflexible and oppressive, both sure they knew what was right, the son fired with a young man's ineluctible certainty, the father appalled almost to the

158

point of tears by the boy's refusal (is he not still a boy?) to understand the world through his eyes, the same eyes that had devoured Federico's mother at the moment of his conception, the eyes that had watched him grow from infant to young manhood.

"You know nothing! *Nothing!*" he would shout. "How could you? You have not lived. You have not struggled. you're not even man enough to be a proper horseman. You don't go out with the other young *cabrones*. Studying, studying, you're always studying. As if that's going to get you anywhere. For God's sake, what's the matter with you?"

Federico would start by answering patiently at first, but later, with the choler of youth, he would point out that it was through laws and intellectual argument that society changed, and not just with feats of machismo or hangings or beatings or pistol shots and ugly threats. "It's what civilisation is for," he would shout, his eyes bright and frightened, jabbing his finger at his enemy like a weapon.

They battled through Federico's late adolescence and early manhood. Don Esteban's disappointment that his son would not don the spurs and leather pants of the ranch-owning *vaquero* was matched by his son's incomprehension of his own father's turpitude.

"What do you think the revolution was for?" he bellowed dramatically, fired with the passion his studies had provoked. "All that fighting, all that death? It was for a constitution, a bill of rights, the law of *amparo* that protects the *campesino* from the landowner, that makes us citizens instead of slaves."

"You naive little boy/young puppy/ignoramus!" his father would shout back choosing his insults apparently at random. "You think laws matter? Laws don't matter. It's power, money, and influence; they're what count here. You can have as many fine words and edicts as you want, but in the end, everything is settled by strong men with banknotes stuffed inside the document they have handed over for processing. The officials cave in. You go to your studies. Go on. Just an excuse to whore and drink as far as I can see. Meanwhile, people like me, the true inheritors of the revolution, will fight our own battles without the help of you lily-livered 'intellectuals'. Shit! That a son of mine would end up being one of them!"

For years, it had hurt badly that his father thought this, and it irritated him profoundly as he got older to realise that the old man was probably right. Money talked all right. It made anything and everything possible, even the contravention of the most idealistic laws. But surely, surely he wanted to scream at his father—as if by shouting hard and long enough he would force him to concede—surely the other way, legal and honourable, was worth fighting for and not through blood sacrifice but through decency and common sense.

As the metro rattled into the stop, Federico was close to tears. He had suddenly realised (again) how much he needed his father's love. No, more than that, he needed his father's approval for the course he had taken. Surely now after all his successes, and because of Angelita, his father accepted him? Perhaps one day they could have that talk, the important one, the one where fathers and sons really compromise.

The phone was ringing as he let himself into the flat, grating on the silence with its sharp teeth, forcing him to drop his battered briefcase and rush to pick up the receiver.

"Papa," was all she said.

"*¡Ay mi hija!* How is it with you? How is your grandfather? Is it bad? Do I come now or can I wait?"

There was a silence at the end of the line. Something was wrong. He could sense it. She was going to tell him—*no!*—that the old man had gone already the inconsiderate old bastard.

"I haven't seen my *abuelo* yet. I haven't even got to San Miguel, Papa." He was suddenly very worried. She was obviously close to tears.

"Child, what's wrong? What's wrong?"

"There's been an accident, Papa. I've been in an accident."

A sound escaped from him, a high-pitched whine, piercing his own heart with love and fear. *Angelita*. What was the world for?

"Papa! Papa! It's all right, that is, I'm all right apart from a few cuts and bruises. They've patched me up here—at the hospital. You'll see, there's nothing wrong, really." But he could hear—because after all he had listened to her all through her childhood—how miserable she was.

"Tell me," he breathed, his pulse raging, a sudden relief flooding through him like some high-kicking drug as he stood awkwardly in the familiar corridor.

He listened to her account of a bus journey that started like any other, and then a breakdown, and of a driver who became furious because he had messed up his clothes with grease and had got delayed as a result. It was bad because he had a wife who was about to give birth (I can't explain now Papi, I'll tell you in a minute), and so he drove too fast and lost control on a curve and the bus smashed a car into the cliffside before flipping over with terrible suddenness.

Federico wanted to reach out and hold his sweet daughter in his arms as he used to do when she had scraped her knee or came back, bullied, from the playground. He wanted to question or shout or cry, but he thrust his fist into his mouth to stop himself. He had to listen. She had to talk—about the wrecked bus, and the imploding windows and the roof buckling as they screamed along the tarmac, and about how when finally the mountain of tin came to a halt and the terrible shrieking of it subsided into an unnatural silence, they heard the sound of a car horn and then people started screaming, sounding like damned creatures in hell. When they managed to crawl out of the wreckage, hands ripping on glass, bags, and other possessions strewn around them, they knew that two people at the front of the bus were dead, and many others were injured. The driver had survived with hardly a scratch.

As they crawled, they were urged on by the passengers of another bus that had stopped to help because that driver had seen, in his mirror, the awful thing that was happening and had immediately turned round to give aid. "Quick, quick!" they shouted, running forward, trying to pull them out. And Angelita kept on talking, the phone burning hot in Federico's hand.

When they were finally standing on the road, away from the wreck, his daughter told him, some of the passengers, the ones not shocked into paralysis of mind and body, started shouting at the driver and saying *it's your fault, you stupid bastard what did you think you were playing at?*

She talked of a gringo—"A really nice guy Papi—who despite

161

having quite obviously broken his leg (and maybe hurt his arm quite badly too), had gone and stood precariously by the man whose actions, it seemed had made this terrible thing happen. Because someone had to protect him. The survivors and their rescuers were ready to tear him limb from limb. One man, blood still pouring from a head cut, had even gone back into the bus wreck to hunt out a piece of rope he'd tied his package with and had, returning, said, 'Come on, this'll do, let's string the *pendejo* up. He deserves it after what he's done.' They all crowded round then," Angelita said. "And they were going to do it. You could feel that they were going to do it.

"The driver, sunglasses hanging broken and awkward from one ear, his face white with shock had started crying then, his words coming out between sobs, *'Dios mío. Dios mío, ten piedad,* have pity on me. I'm sorry, I'm sorry I thought it was OK, I never meant... I thought I'd make it, oh please please, I didn't want to hurt anyone, I just wanted to—my wife. A baby. *Dios mío,* what have I done? Help me, help me.'

"But the passengers, bloodied and enraged, faces puckered with retributive zeal, just jeered at him and moved forward, death in their hearts, murder in their eyes. And that's when Martin, Papi, that's the name of the *gringo,* that's when he started talking, shouting at everyone in the middle of that, well you know Papi, it's like a wilderness there, and he said, 'There's been enough death here already. Surely you must see that.'

"And all the time, Papi, he was in terrible pain, I could see that, but he kept on. 'This isn't the way to do things," he said. 'Maybe this man was going too fast, yes, he was going too fast, but he didn't actually intend to kill anyone did he? He didn't say, hey I want to murder the man in that little old taxi, hey I really want to do away with some of my passengers. He was careless, reckless, God, I'm sure we all know that, but to murder him in cold blood! You'd never forgive yourselves later. Death is too final, too terrible for that.'

"I'm not sure they really listened to what he was saying Papi, I'm not sure I did, but he kept going, just kept going, talking them down, saying, 'once death has happened, once you know you've had a part in someone else's death, well it hangs on you like a rotten poncho. It's like a great dragging weight of shame, God.. I know I'm a foreigner and I'm sorry to be talking like this to all of you, but it's just that there are laws, a whole society to deal with this, but not us. Not us, now when we're all so—God it hurts... It's not, we're not, please, please, I implore you.'

"Then Papi, he just sort of turned and collapsed there in the road. It was so awful. But he'd succeeded, you see, because everyone just moved away a bit, backed off, and left the driver standing there on his own while we all sat or hung around at the side of the road and then a mobile went off and helicopters arrived, ambulances, the police. And that driver, Papi, his life is over too, isn't it? He'll be in prison forever. And his wife? What a mess."

"Oh Angelita, poor Angelita, are you…"

"I came to the hospital with Martin, Papi, because I was so proud of him. He almost reminded me of you. No, don't get offended or anything, he's not like you really, too soft or something. I got talking to him. On the coach you see. That's how I know. At least I think I do."

Know what? he wanted to ask.

"So you see, Papi, I haven't got to my *abue's* house yet. I'm sorry. I love you, Papi. Have I told you that? Have I ever told you that enough?"

She was crying now. He could hear her sobbing down the line. He must have been standing in the corridor for hours.

"Yes, child," he whispered. "You have told me that. Often. It is one of the things that makes my life worth living." He could hardly contain his own tears now. "Listen," he gasped. "I'll come and get you, then we'll go on together."

"No Papi," she replied. "No. I'll wait here with Martin. I'll help him on the bus to San Miguel when he's properly plastered up. Tomorrow. I'll get there tomorrow, Papi. You catch a plane. Or something. In case. You know."

He knew. What if his father had already died? What if he never regained consciousness enough for his son to be able to say (because it was true) what his own daughter had just told him?

"Get there soon Angelita," he said. "If you're sure you're all

163

right? And Angelita, my love, I love you too, you know that, and what I think I'll do, I'll get a taxi to the airport right now. See if I can get a seat on the late flight or hang around for the early morning plane. There's something I have to tell your grandfather, the old bastard."

Jacinto

AFTER HIS LAST STUDENT—A not very talented young man with thick glasses and a lisp, whose bowing still lacked fluidity—had gone, smarting from his teacher's unkind words and damning criticism, Professor Jacinto Perez packed his violin carefully into its case, checked that he had the scores he needed for the forthcoming concert and rang for Salvador, the school's general all-round everything, to come and get his cases and tell Manuel, the driver, to bring the car because he needed to get to the airport.

He didn't need to go to San Miguel for another couple of days really. There would still be time for rehearsal if he put off travelling for a bit longer. He knew the state orchestra had played the Symphony of a Hundred Moments three times in the last two years so the players presumably felt comfortable with the notes. The Double Concerto was a standard component of any band's repertoire and the overture—well—players grew up with that. So no, he didn't really need to go up just yet. The day before the concert would have been fine. But he had to get out of the house. His wife was becoming more distant by the hour and Francisco was puffing up like some kind of emotional balloon. A huge pressure was building up so that pretty soon unless something was done, he was going to erupt in a great hail of accusations and adolescent turmoil.

165

If only he knew what to say to the boy. But he could find no means to broach the subject. His relationship with his son was far too precarious for him to take him to one side and say, 'Look son, it's just the kind of thing that happens, nothing to worry about, no need to trouble your mother about it.' His son would need more than that, much more.

Yes, these things happen, they had to happen sometimes, nothing to them really, honestly son, son. Then why was he haunted by the memory of the girl, the way her body lay in that pre-door-opening bliss, the curve of her abdomen, her eyes, the touch, the feel of her when he, when they—stop it, stop it, he ordered himself, don't think about it. You've done this kind of thing before. I didn't have trouble letting go before. But something about Angelita was special. Perhaps it was just the way it had turned out, the mess of Francisco's interruption. Maybe it was the unease he felt about the boy or the fact that the young violinist had stopped coming to class —not difficult to divine the reason—and who she might have told.

If his colleagues found out, there'd be a scandal. Newspapers even, maybe. The whole thing. Yet if he could just talk to her, apologise, ask for her understanding, tell her the story of his life, and who he was, she might save him, and then, who knows, he could reach her again, pour his skill into her, watch the swing of her forearm, cup her hand in his, feel her breath against his cheek. He shook his head, sucked in his breath, and grimaced to try and drive the images away.

His driver said as he opened the door for the great maestro Perez, "Sir, are you all right?"

Jacinto, realising how he must have looked in the midst of his confusion, quickly controlled himself and said, "Of course, just an old memory," which of course it was. Ridiculous.

He kept thinking about it as they drove to the airport. Manuel soon realised that he was not in the mood for talk. Jacinto Perez knew himself to be in the grip of temporary madness, and, when he got his mind back from time to time, he was quite self-aware enough to know that he was in trouble and that his young ex-student, beautiful and talented though she was had no real part in his life story— unless, that is, she was to be the catalyst for some catastrophic change in his situation. His fantasies about her were just fantasies. Nothing more. All he had to do was to forget her. All she had to do was to keep her mouth shut. Life would get back to normal. Then again, if he found the boys! If he could only find the boys...

"Sorry, Professor, you said?"

"What? What did I say?"

"Something about finding the boys. Sir?"

"Oh no. Nothing. Sorry, Manuel. Didn't realise I'd spoken aloud."

Leave me alone, Señorita Angelita, he said to her in his own mind. *Get on with your own life. I promise I won't bother you again.* He closed his eyes against the city's illuminated evening, trying to conjure up his wife's mysterious eyes and the pleasure he would feel when he walked through her door with his boys, her twins, but all he could see was the sparkle in Angelita's eyes, all he could hear was a door opening and a groan.

At the airport, he felt better, grateful for the noise of it all. He called a porter to take his bags but held on to his violin, clutching it to himself like a boy's toy when the man tried to put it on to the trolley with the other bags. He said goodbye to Manuel and followed his suitcases to the first-class desk where he was treated with efficient deference. In the VIP lounge, he agreed to the barman's suggestion and had a large whisky and soda until finally, after downing it rather quickly, he was able to stop pacing around.

He concentrated on the music he was to play and conduct. He called to mind the look of the pieces as they appeared on the page. He studied the colours and pictures the notes made in his imagination. He wondered just how much he dared exaggerate the rubato in the slow movement of the concerto. Would that young Julio be able to cope with it? He thought about what he would say to the orchestra about the overture, how he would get them to explode into its carnival grandiloquence with light and passion, energy and re-purposed enthusiasm.

When he got onto the plane, he was ushered aboard with barely concealed sycophancy by the captain himself who stood at the cockpit door to shake his hand. His equilibrium was properly restored. He always got a window seat because he liked to rest his

167

head on the thin aircraft skin when he wasn't staring out, looking for music of the spheres in the tropospheric spaces they travelled in. By the time he had clicked on his seat belt and accepted the first glass of complimentary champagne, he had almost started to look forward to the trip, to seeing that nice Marisol again, to making music, and to being loved.

Behind him, the cabin crew were going up and down the aisle slamming overhead lockers in a percussion of metal and plastic as the bins locked shut. Everyone was seated. It was clear they were about to depart. He watched the familiar preparations lazily, letting the whisky and the champagne think for him.

A member of the crew started to close the main door, but then stopped and pushed it back open again to let a final passenger come running and panting into the cabin. To Jacinto's surprise—seeing that the man was wearing a very ordinary and slightly shabby suit with his tie pulled carelessly from his throat—the late arrival made straight for his row and sat down in the seat next to him. He was clutching an old briefcase and a crumpled holdall.

"*¡Madre!*" he exhaled, his head on the seat rest, breathing heavily with sweat standing out on his cheeks. "I thought I wasn't going to make it."

"They usually hold the plane back for as long as possible. For us," the professor replied. He could smell the man's sweat, the stink of burnt tobacco smoke on his breath.

"Us? Oh I see! You mean first-class passengers? It's my first time. I wouldn't have done it normally. Not my style, even if I could afford it. But it was the only ticket I could get to San Miguel tonight so I had to—an emergency. Two emergencies, actually."

Professor Jacinto Perez grunted in acknowledgement that he had heard, and then closed his eyes for rest, and as a sign that he did not want to continue the conversation. He could almost feel the disappointment of the man beside him.

The plane left the gate and rumbled toward the runway. Jacinto was pleasantly oblivious of their uneven progress, floating in and out of consciousness, his head full of music and sons, the greetings of the cabin crew, and the whine of flaps and ailerons as the pilots checked the plane. Yet there was something familiar about the person who had arrived at his side.

Later, having experienced take-off and climb in his half-conscious state, he was dragged back to wakefulness by the voice of a member of the cabin staff. "Professor Perez, Professor Perez, do you want a snack, some more champagne perhaps, a cocktail?" It took him a little time to work out where he was and how to respond. He lifted his heavy lids and thought, in a moment of lucidity, that it would be better to arrive in a more or less sober state.

"Orange juice?" he asked. "Is that possible? A big one—with ice?" He didn't feel in top form. It was the doze he'd just had, or perhaps the weeks of stress.

"Professor Perez!" the man next to him exclaimed. "I thought I recognised you. You're the violinist, aren't you, from the music school?"

"Well yes, I do play the violin, that is true."

"My daughter, she's a student of yours. We met, briefly, you probably won't remember. It was at the end-of-semester concert last June."

Jacinto suddenly knew who the man was.

"You're my daughter's teacher. My daughter—Angelita Hernandez Remedios."

"Ah, yes," he gulped, trying to re-establish himself "Angelita! Yes! She is my student. Of course."

"Is she any good?" Federico asked. "I mean I know she was good enough to get into her school. But is she really good?"

"Well, yes, I think she has considerable talent." How had fate done this to him, when he was trying so hard to get rid of her?

"Maestro, I'm sorry to ask you this, but have you noticed anything strange about her recently? She seems a bit low to me, a bit distracted. I've tried to get her to tell me what the problem is, I'm her father after all, but she just says nothing's wrong. But a parent knows. Something's not quite right, I'm sure."

He obviously doesn't know she's been skipping school, Jacinto realised. What should I do then? With any other parent I'd point out that their child was playing truant, but with her—I can't say anything.

"I can't say I've noticed anything special," he said, hoping his lie would not come back to haunt him, "but I'll see what I can find out, OK?" He hoped that would finish the conversation. It was most uncomfortable.

"She's been in a coach crash, poor child. She was on her way to see her grandfather."

"What?" the violin teacher exclaimed, "What did you say? A crash? Little Angelita? She is hurt? I pray to God she is not hurt." He was suddenly panic-stricken by the thought of her injured, and then immediately terrified that he had given himself away.

"It does you credit that you care so much for your pupils," Angelita's father said and proceeded to tell the startled musician what he knew, not excepting his own father's demise, the reason for the journeys in the first place.

This meant that when they landed at San Miguel some forty minutes later, Jacinto had to offer the man a lift in the car that had been sent to meet him. Federico started to decline. "I'll get a taxi'," he said, but the professor knew he was obliged to extend this politeness. He pressed him, and when Angelita's father accepted the offer, the two men set off together on the long ride from the airport to the city of San Miguel.

They arrived at Jacinto's hotel. The professor exited, and his bags were taken from the limousine by the hotel porter.

"Take this man wherever he needs to go," he told the driver. He said goodbye to the girl's father and walked into reception.

"Ah, Professor," the man behind the desk greeted him. "May I say what a pleasure it is to have you with us?"

"Thank you," Jacinto countered, feeling less sociable than he was forced to appear, and still smarting from the agony of having to deal with Angelita's father. "You have a room for me, I believe."

"Of course sir. You'll be in the double, I suppose?"

"The double? I don't understand."

"Yes sir. I'm sorry sir, they did try to reserve the suite for you, but I'm afraid that it had already been booked for the duration of the festival. Don't worry, the executive rooms are really magnificent. We already had the best one reserved for you. Then your wife rang to book a single, too."

He wasn't sure he was hearing correctly. "My wife?" he said. "My wife? Why would she ring about that? My room was booked by Marisol Cardova, wasn't it?"

"Yes sir, of course, but your wife rang early this morning to make some changes. She said you might be surprised, but that you'd be pleased." He beamed at the startled musician. "I've put you and the señora in room 1052, and the young Mr Perez in room 1053. They have connecting doors."

He would have contested the man's information, but he was too shocked. Marisa—here? Francisco? Good God, that's what he'd come to escape. How could they do this to him? It ruined everything. He couldn't think straight. What were they doing here? Why were they coming? Perhaps they were here already. What on earth was going on? First the girl's father, now this! He thought he would faint with the shock of it. Damn! Damn!

He took the key from the receptionist and turned without looking toward the lift. He failed to notice the bellman standing patiently with the trolley loaded with his bags. His left foot caught one of the trolley wheels and distracted as he was, he didn't manage to compensate for the sudden loss of forward mobility. His legs went from under him and he fell onto the hotel's marble floor.

At the last moment, a reflex took over and he put his right hand out in front of him to break his fall. Which it did, taking his weight at such an awkward angle that something had to give, however small. Even if it was just his little finger.

He felt the snap of bone. The pain came later. He was aware of the tearing of tendons in the two fingers next to it. As he lay in the foyer, humiliated, people ran to help him. All he could think was, *My life has suddenly slipped right out of my control.* Then, as he was helped to struggle to his feet, *I can't play the violin if the fingers of my bowing hand are damaged in this way. What on earth am I going to do now?*

Juan

EVEN THOUGH HE hardly knew where he was or what he was doing here, Juan ordered another shot of Blanquita, paid too much for it, and tipped it down his throat. So what if he couldn't taste anymore? It didn't make him feel any better, but then he wasn't really feeling anything, drowning, as he was in misery, self-pity, inchoate anger, and incomprehension. He didn't even notice that the other clients in the squalid little room that served as a bar had been avoiding him all evening not just because of the way he looked, all hollow-eyed, unshaven, and apparently ready for homelessness, but also because of the fetid aroma that surrounded him. Juan had gone to pieces and somewhere, deep down, he knew this and that just made it worse which is why, of course, he needed another drink.

Was it Maria that had made him feel this way? Because he loved her? Or perhaps hated her? Or was it, perhaps, because of his humiliation, reducing him to the size he was, not the person he had once aspired to be? That day, as she had walked away from him amongst the metal and exhaust, horns blaring while he was stuck, marooned, and impotent, he had to accept that he was as powerless as he had feared.

Their little apartment was empty now. Maria was not around to organise his life. Even though he had resented it every second of every day, he seemed to be incapable of doing it himself.

"This isn't what I wanted!" he screamed. "I wanted love and hope and fresh air and sunrises and a decent salary to live on and children. I wanted children. But what I got instead was no money and clouds of smog and a need to escape. And no children. I spend my days scratching a living on the crowded roads in the filthy air fighting all that metal and rubber and wondering how much longer my old rust bucket of a taxi will last. It's been stuck back together so many times that it is about the fall apart."

And then there was his *vecina* Esmeralda, whose mock sympathetic concern was, he knew, simply a mask for the scorn with which she viewed him. He could see the disgust in her face as he started drinking heavily, stopped taking care of himself, and, to be frank, lost whatever habits of personal hygiene he had once practised.

Somehow, he managed to make it home from the bar, falling over only once. He didn't notice when he grazed his knee quite badly. Somehow he made it up the stone stairs to the little flat, crawled to the bed, and fell unconscious on top of an untidy pile of used clothes.

The next thing he knew was that someone was shaking him. "Juan, Juan *despierta*," a voice was shrieking. *Wake up wake up.*

God, his insides felt like a compost heap and his knee hurt like *la mierda*. On top of that, Esmeralda's harsh voice was truly horrible. When he tried to open his eyes, the lids were too heavy to lift and the light seared into his eyeballs. He wanted to go back to sleep.

Juan, Juan, wake up, for the love of God man, wake up and do something about yourself. You look terrible and you stink. Get some water and wash yourself.

He turned away from her and closed his eyes. But that didn't work. She was shaking him by the shoulder. "Juan, you feeling bad? Well of course you do, *¿verdad?* I'm not surprised the way you've been behaving. You should be ashamed." She stopped. But then she was off again. "It's time for you to do something, time to make all this come right again. Like it was. Like it has to be. She shook him again. Come on. Juan. Juan. Get up *idiota!*"

He groaned.

173

"Come on. Wake up. Get up".

He rolled over, and somehow managed to sit. His head hung low and he couldn't look up.

"That's better," his neighbour said. "Now come on and get up. Wash yourself, for heaven's sake. Find some clean clothes. If you have any. Then come and see me. I have something to tell you, something you will want to know, and something you are going to do something about."

He groaned again. She sailed out of the room, slamming the door behind her. That hurt. He tried to shake the tumbleweed from his brain, but his mouth was dry and his eyes stung. He got to his feet and staggered to the bathroom. He thought he was going to be sick. He had never felt so awful. He stood over the sink and gulped down two large tumblers of water, completely forgetting to get it from the *garafón* that stood in the corner with its purified contents.

He took off his stinking shirt and dumbly, with limbs that could hardly function, washed himself as best he could. He sorted through the clothes that were piled all over the flat and found a pair of underpants that seemed cleaner than the others. He pulled on trousers and a crumpled shirt and put on his customary huaraches. He splashed water in his hair and tried to plaster it into some kind of order in the cracked mirror in front of him. His eyes were dull and bloodshot, he realised, and he had a few days' stubble growth on his chin. He should shave. He couldn't face shaving.

He drank some more water and shuffled out of the flat. He knocked on Doña Esmeralda's door. When she opened it, she stood and looked at him. "You look, like…" words failed her. "I suppose it will have to do. But for the love of God wash your mouth out. Your breath..!" She made a gesture and turned away.

Then she told Juan that Maria was going with the rich *gringa* to San Miguel de las Colinas. She told him what to do if he wanted to get her back.

"You are her husband. It is your obligation to have her back with you. It is her duty to be here." Doña Esmeralda was all schoolmistress. "If you want her back," she told him, "if you are a man, you should follow them and make her come back with you."

So he was behind the wheel, the taxi rattling along the *carretera* out of the city. Modern cars flashed past on his left, great trucks thundered behind him, blaring their horns, and long-distance buses, diesel engines roaring, heading off to towns and cities all over the republic screamed past him.

The air was clearer now, and the hills on either side of the motorway looked greener and fresher than when you only saw them through the contaminated air of the city.

Every now and then, the engine of the taxi would cough and splutter. Once, he thought it would fail completely, and then what would he do? The light hurt his eyes and the almost defunct shock absorbers delivered every bump on the tarmac directly up his spine. Added to this, he was incredibly tired and feared he might fall asleep at the wheel. He was seething with resentment about how life was treating him and furious with his bitch of a wife who was putting him through this. Just because he got a bit cross with her sometimes. But surely she knew he loved her really, the stupid woman.

Against his wishes, a few minutes later, his eyes closed. When he opened them he was already heading to the edge of the motorway, about to crash into the side barrier. His sudden panic shocked him back awake. He desperately wrenched the wheel to avoid almost certain death. The worn tyres of the old taxi screeched in protest.

He knew he was in danger of falling asleep again. As soon as he could, he got off the highway and parked by the side of a small country road. His head slipped down on his chest and he fell deeply asleep in an instant. Although he was completely unconscious, something was happening to him. Images and flickers of scenes that might have been real but which seemed to exist in some other fantasy world fluttered around his brain and when he woke up a few minutes later, refreshed and suddenly alive, it was with the sense of a great light being shone upon him.

It wasn't as if his head was clear of the ravages of alcoholic dehydration or that his body had completely forgotten the poison he had poured into it, but in some way, he felt purified as if some vision had been granted him. He looked around him as if the source of this wonderment would be found somewhere outside the windows of the taxi. Of course, there was nothing, but he had a strong sense that something important had happened.

Bewildered and amazed, he stepped out of the taxi and went behind one of the two black Zapote trees at the side of the road. His knee really hurt, but that only served to elevate his sense of wonder. He relieved himself. As he made his way back to the old cab, he had the oddest feeling. If he had been able to put it into words he might have called it *hope*.

He stretched and breathed in the fresh air, conscious of the hum of the motorway a kilometre away. Things seemed different now, but what was, actually, different? He couldn't wait to tell Maria about this, the strangest and most beautiful thing that had happened to him. Of course, he told himself, it could be the effects of all the drinking but it didn't feel like that. It felt like—but he couldn't really say what it felt like, just that it was good and the dark cloud of self-loathing had suddenly been lifted from him.

He got back into the taxi and gunned the starter motor, but nothing happened. Normally he would have uttered a profanity at this familiar occurrence, but now he just chuckled and tried again. The third time the old engine spluttered into life and once he had managed to lift the brake handle clear before letting it flop back down he was ready to go. He looked up and down the road. Seeing no one, he turned back and started out the way he had come and once on the motorway again he suddenly found himself humming and half singing one of the corridas he had enjoyed as a young man.

As he drove along, he started to think about what he would say to Maria when he found her. He was sure he would. He wouldn't shout at her, he wouldn't *regañar* her—tell her off. How could he, after everything? For he saw things differently now. He had been transfigured. Away from their fetid flat and the city stink, away from the acid corrosion of their neighbour, and the disappointment (as he saw it) of his life, he felt refreshed in the sunshine and the panorama that stretched before him.

He thought of the way he had treated his wife. He was full of shame and disgust. But he was also comforted by the knowledge that he could make it all better. Once he told her how he felt and why he had been driven to take out all his frustrations on her, she would understand, surely. It was just that he had been so unhappy and then, well, what was he to do? OK, he admitted to himself, maybe that wasn't quite right. He had behaved badly but it wasn't too late to do something about it.

In this spirit of elevated expectation, as if just by thinking he could be purged, Juan drove onwards. He stopped for a Coke and tamales, and he consumed them with joy. He carried onwards toward the light of his salvation.

He left the highway and found himself climbing into the hills. The road snaked and curved and the taxi groaned in protest as it leant into the curves. Buses roared past him in both directions. Even for a driver of his experience, it was quite a challenge to keep the old car on the road. Once he worried that the brakes weren't holding up. This alarmed him. Yet even this thought failed to dampen the ridiculous sense of joy that seemed to have overtaken him. Had he been more self-aware, he might have tried to analyse what was happening, but lacking the ability for analytic reflection, his heart just sang and all his guilt was washed away in the joyful resolution that awaited him.

In the rearview mirror he saw an intercity bus approaching at speed.

"*¡Dios mío!*" he muttered. "He's crazy going that fast."

The bus was at his back bumper. As they approached a sharp bend, it pulled out to overtake him. *He must be insane*, thought the taxi driver, imagining that someone could be coming the other way.

He saw the high sides of the vehicle alongside him. He clutched the steering wheel tightly to keep the taxi on the road.

The roar of the diesel was loud in his ear. Then he saw it. Another bus suddenly was coming in the other lane. There was going to be a collision. There was no avoiding it.

Luckily for Juan, it all happened so quickly that he had no time to be afraid. He was concentrating too hard on his survival to have time for fear.

There was a roar in his ears, a blaring of horns, and then the bus that was overtaking him careered towards him.

The bus's rear-end made shocking contact with the taxi as it lurched over and fell onto the road.

In a screaming shriek of despair, squashing him flat in an instant.

He never felt a thing.

Cast of Characters

In order of appearance

- *Anselmo Gonzalez de Luna,* a retired seller of toys
- *Martin Caldecott,* a language teacher, translator, and writer; a brother of Vicky
- *Maria Moreno Cochinaba,* a maid married to Juan; she works for Vicky
- *Jacinto Perez, a* music professor and violinist married to Marisa; the father of the twins and Francisco
- *Angelita Hernandez Remedios,* a music student; a daughter of Federico
- *Victoria Kassoniliki (Bicky),* a radio presenter, married to Alexei; a sister of Martin
- *Federico Hernandez Placencia,* a son of Don Estaban; the father of Angelita
- *Don Estaban,* a landowner, brother of Tia Rosario; the father of Federico
- *Tia Rosario,* a sister of Don Estaban
- *Marcelita,* a woman with learning difficulties; a daughter of Tia Rosario
- *Marisa Sepulveda de Perez,* a singer, married to Jacinto
- *The twins,* sons of Jacinto and Marisa, brothers of Francisco

- *Francisco Perez,* a student; a son of Jacinto and Marisa
- *Julio Delgadillo Aceves,* a music student; a brother of Genoveva
- *Marisol Cardova,* a festival organiser and one-time lover of Jacinto
- *Alexei Kassoniliki,* a vulcanologist; he is married to Victoria
- *Genoveva Delgadillo Aceves,* a nurse; a sister of Julio
- *Don Venustiano Heredia,* a landowner
- *Silvestre Ocampo,* the *alcalde* (mayor) of San Miguel de las Colinas
- *Silverio Plat* (no 22), a leader of the EAS
- *Dr Martinez,* a member of the EAS
- *The Sons of Perpetual Light,* a quasi-religious sect led by the 'Halo'
- *Ejercito de Arturo Sanchez (EAS),* a left-wing protest group

About the Author

Jeremy Harmer is well known for his books about the teaching of English as a foreign language —or books directly aimed at students of English themselves. He has also, for many years, been a writer of fiction titles. He has worked in Mexico and the UK, in New York (online for the New School) and elsewhere. He has worked with teachers all over the world and addressed many conferences. Aside from the teaching of English Jeremy is also a practicing musician and singer-songwriter and has released four CDs.

About the Series

Look for volumes two and three in the *Volcano at San Miguel* series.

Old Gods, to be published late 2023.

Burning Questions, to be published in 2024.